THE LAST ROAD TRIP

THE LAST ROAD TRIP

JAMES ELSENER

This is a work of fiction. All the names, characters, places, organizations, institutions, and events portrayed in this novel are products of the author's imagination. Any similarity to real persons, living or dead, is coincidental and not intended by the author.

ISBN 978-1-7325233-0-2 (print)
ISBN 978-1-7325233-1-9 (ebook)

Cover design by Carrie Dockendorff, Arlington Heights, IL
Book design by Marueen Cutajar, gopublished.com

CHAPTER

1

My nine-year major league career came to an end on October 2, the last day of the season before 4,267 shivering fans in Cleveland's Progressive Field when I grounded out to the second baseman. That's probably the wimpiest out in baseball. He threw me out by six feet. The game had started at 1:10 p.m. and was over by 3:15, just over two hours. We all wanted to get a long sad season over with.

I made the last out of the last game of the year. And the last game of my career. We finished 27 games out of first place. There weren't any playoffs for us. This was it. We played out the schedule to entertain the few remaining fans who wanted to be there at the end or were out of work and didn't have anything else to do that day. We finished the season playing the Royals three games at home. They were 25 ½ games out. The total attendance for the series didn't total 20,000. Who wants to see two clubs at the bottom of the standings on the last weekend of the season?

The club had notified me in August that it wasn't going to pick up my option for the next season and I figured it was just as well. After 16 years of bouncing around professional baseball I had come to the same conclusion, that it was time to have a real life. When you enter professional sports, you know the time will come when you have to hang it up, but while you are living the life you just put that day of reckoning back into the deep recesses of your mind. Now I had to face it.

As I walked back to the dugout I tried to take in all the sounds and sights around me. There was little chance that I would ever come back as a coach or a manager. That part of the business never really appealed to me. That just wasn't my thing. So, I knew this would be the last time I would smell the grass and hear the chatter of the vendors and the fans, even though at that moment most of them were just trying to stay warm while they filed out of the empty stadium. We could feel winter beginning to creep up on us.

Over the years that I had been in the game, something always pulled me to visit ballparks during the winter off-season when the grass was dormant and brown and snow covered the seats and the aisles. It always looked so forlorn, sort of the same way I was feeling at that moment.

"Hey, Hoss. Good swing. Good swing." Charlie Barlow was our manager. He was a baseball lifer and one of the better guys in the game. He always found something positive even in a groundout to second by a player who was retiring immediately after the game was over. But after you finish in last place two years in a row he knew he would be coaching young pitchers in Bluefield next year.

Charlie had played me that day as a favor. It was my last opportunity to be on a big-league field. I hadn't played all that much down the stretch with the team giving a good look to the younger players who would form their roster next year.

"Stub, you want to play left field today?" he asked me shortly after I had arrived at the stadium. During my career I had been primarily a third baseman with medium power at the bat. But one reason I had stayed in the majors with four teams as long as I had was my ability to play other positions, such as first base and the outfield. I even filled in as a catcher on a few occasions.

"Sure, Charlie. That would be great. Thanks." Neither one of us had to say anything about this being my last day in the big leagues. I got one hit in four at bats, a single to right field off a rookie pitcher named David Hobbs, who in my opinion would be back in Triple A next year and probably never see the big leagues again. He didn't have much oomph on his fastball and his breaking pitches were more like slurves. There was nothing sharp about anything he threw.

But, like Moonlight Graham, at least he would get his name in the Baseball Encyclopedia and be able to tell people back home about his days pitching with the Royals. He probably wouldn't talk much about giving up the last career hit of an average major leaguer named Kenny Rowe, better known as Stub.

I finished my career with a .268 batting average. As a corner infielder I had to have some power to stay in the lineup. I averaged more than 20 home runs a year, ending with 191 round-trippers and 765 RBIs. Not hall of fame stats but nothing to be ashamed of. I got to the World Series once with the Cardinals. We lost in six games to the Yankees that year, but I had two hits in seven at bats. I even made the All-Star team one year when I was second in the league in home runs by the end of June. Fortunately, the fan voting was based on the first half of the season because after the break I had a total of five home runs to go with the 19 I had before the break.

By the time I reached the dugout, most of my teammates had already headed for the locker room. They were anxious to pack up and head home after a long season of losing. Losing breeds losing and most of us could feel it back in late May when we had been around the league once and knew we didn't have the firepower to compete with the top teams.

The equipment managers were packing up the bats and the other equipment not taken by the players. The Gatorade jug and the trash, empty paper cups, discarded tobacco and gum wrappers would be the responsibility of the stadium maintenance crew.

I'm not sure what I was thinking at this time. I was just going through the end of the game motions. This wasn't the normal end of the season when I would already be thinking how next year I would improve – fewer strikeouts, more hits to the opposite field, anxious to face that pitcher again who got me out on a 3-2 curve ball when I was looking for a fastball in. I would never have that chance again.

When I reached the locker room I noted the amount of trash the guys were throwing toward the buckets that were set in the middle of the room. Balls of wadded up old tape were shot at the trash cans as if they were basketballs. Nobody bothered to pick them up when they missed. Other discarded items were old toiletries, game programs and equipment that needed to be replaced next year. The locker room attendants had all winter to clean the room.

Usually there was care given to the clubhouse. This was our place of business and our home where we spent a lot of time before, during and after games. Right now, all anyone wanted to do was get out of there. Half of them probably wouldn't be back in Cleveland next year. This was one of those years that management would definitely "back up the truck," as the old baseball saying goes.

A couple of the newspaper and wire service beat reporters were in the room looking for year-end stories from a last-place team. Andy Oyler, a hair-sprayed TV reporter from WZXB, was cruising with his camera crew trying to get a few one-liners for the 11 p.m. newscast. No one was in much of a mood to talk.

I sat down on the stool in my stall and slowly undressed. I took a shot at the trash can with a ball of tape that I had taken off a pad I had strapped to my elbow where I had been hit earlier in the year. I missed.

"Stub, you want to come over for dinner tonight? I think we're going to do burgers on the grill. Nothing fancy." Frank Laporte was my best friend on the team. Even though we were about the same age, he probably had a few years left pitching out of the bullpen. He was one of those guys who learned to throw without putting a lot of stress on his arm. During his career he had only been on the disabled list once, and that was for a broken toe he had suffered when he tripped over the top step of the dugout.

We had first played with each other at Quad Cities in the Low-A Midwest League. Like most baseball careers we had gone in different directions and often found ourselves facing each other before ending up in Cleveland together again. Even though we hadn't discussed it directly, he knew this was my last day in the big leagues.

"Thanks, Frank. That sounds like a good idea. What can I bring? What time do you want me there?"

"Sevenish will do. Just bring yourself. Everything else is on Jill and me."

Frank had married Jill Martin when they were in Triple-A Indianapolis. She had worked for the team in marketing and knew what she had signed for up by marrying a baseball player.

She was one of the good wives in the game who knew how to take care of the family, the house and the finances while her husband was on the road half the year. Even when he was home it was like being on the road. Most of his waking hours were spent at the ballpark. Of course, the money is good and that takes care of a lot of the issues and holds some marriages together at least until retirement.

Frank had hit the jackpot with Jill and he knew it. I had always had my own crush on her and rarely turned down an invitation to their house. They were a couple that was always fun to be around.

"I need to head upstairs to get a few things taken care of," I told Frank. "I'll catch you over at your house." By the time I had showered and shaved the locker room was almost empty. Charlie and a couple of the coaches were in his office having a beer and a cigar. They would all be looking for other jobs next year.

I dressed, put a few remaining items from my stall into my duffel bag and went over to say my goodbyes. We all wished each other well. We weren't friends, necessarily; in fact, there were a couple of the coaches I really couldn't stand. Bob Tacker had a career in the major leagues for all of one week and he was still bitter about it. He was not pleasant to be around. I never could figure out how Charlie, whose personality was totally opposite, had him on his staff. I guess it was just a case of yin and yang. Good cop and bad cop.

The GM's office was about a five-minute walk from the locker room through a matrix of hallways that snaked through the underbelly of the stadium. Emptying stadiums always have that sound of clacking seats and a few loud drunk voices from the guys that didn't know it was time to leave. The only way I was ever going to hear that again would be to buy a ticket and stay through the end of the game.

Janet Starkovich was sitting at her extremely neat desk that guarded the entrance to the management suites. She was in her late 40s, almost 6 feet tall with the body of someone who goes to the gym daily. Despite the fact that she was probably at least 20 years older than most of the players, she was considered a "hottie." But that didn't keep her from serving as a den mother to the team. She knew everyone involved with the team and how to get things done behind the scenes. She had started with the team shortly after college as an intern. She had seen several hundred players come and go. She knew they were commodities but always kept a professional relationship between herself and "the boys."

"Hi, Stub. Nice hit today. A few feet to the left and you could have gone for two. Looking for Elton?"

"Yep. Is he in?"

"Let me check. He was in a meeting a few minutes ago."

I waited patiently in the reception area. Other than for the baseball motif decorating the walls, I could just as well have been waiting in the offices of an insurance company or any other business for that matter. After about 5 minutes the phone rang on Janet's desk and she gave me the go ahead.

Elton Woodard had been GM in Cleveland for 6 years, a run which had produced zero playoff appearances, declining attendance and a farm system that was ranked 28th out of the 30 major league teams by the industry trade publication Baseball America.

Elton would probably also find a seat on the truck this year and would be selling real estate by the time spring training began.

"Hello, Kenneth." He always called me by my formal name. As always Elton was dressed in a suit with a bow tie. We figured he wanted to look like the immortal Branch Rickey. He certainly had the rotund shape of Rickey and, so far, his performance as a GM did resemble Rickey's in his latter days with the last-place Pittsburgh Pirates rather than when his teams were winning pennants in St. Louis and Brooklyn. Elton had never had this winning streak.

"Elton, I just wanted to stop up and say goodbye, wish everyone the best. Not sure where I'll be next year, but I wanted to thank you for giving me another year in the league."

I had learned over the years never to burn bridges. I had seen bitter old ballplayers who had reached the end of the line burn everyone in their path as they went out the door for the last time. Some of them couldn't even get a free game ticket after that.

"Ever need a job, son, give me a call. I have lots of contacts. You always seemed to work well with the younger players. Let Janet know where we can reach you."

Probably every player thinks about staying in the game as a coach or manager. Usually that meant having to start all over again in Pocatello riding the buses with 19-year-olds, keeping them from drinking, beating off and throwing out their arms on a 40-degree night in the Northwest League. All major league players like to talk about their experiences coming up as if it was the best time in their life, but few of us really want to go back there.

"I haven't decided what to do, Elton. I think I just need a little time off to weigh some possibilities. I'll figure it out."

"I'm sure you will. I'm sure you will." Elton was thinking more about his future than he was mine at that moment. He held out his hand and said "good luck." This was the ritual he had performed hundreds of times during his years in baseball as the revolving roster door never stopped spinning.

Baseball mathematics is this - there are only 200 members enshrined in the Baseball Hall of Fame. More than 17,000 have played in the major leagues. Multiply that number by at least 10 to get the number of those that signed a professional contract but never got out of the minors. It's no wonder that baseball executives don't look at us as anything special. Replacing us is easy. It's that search for the one or two stars that feeds the dreams of scouts and top management.

One baseball team owner described the task of filling out his minor league rosters as having "one legitimate player and eight guys for him to play catch with." Once we make it to the major leagues, most of us recognize early on that we are nothing special.

I figure Elton was really thinking "Don't let the door hit you in the ass on the way out."

I made sure Janet had my current e-mail, cell number and the address of the apartment I had rented for the year in Shaker Heights. I still had five months to go on the lease, so I wasn't planning on moving immediately. I would eventually have to think about a permanent address.

My ex-wife Loretta lived with our two kids in what was once "our" house in suburban Chicago. I had spent four years with the White Sox. We liked it there and it seemed to be a good place to put down roots. When in-between official addresses, which I usually was, I had mail sent there and used it as my residence of record. Loretta was cool with that. We divorced without animosity. We just got tired of each other. Our marriage was a victim of life in baseball. I was never home and when I was, I was never home. We have a son, Scotty, who is now 7 and a daughter, Nicole, 5. I will have to make a trip to Chicago to see them.

Loretta had not remarried but I knew she was seeing someone and the thought of that guy, no matter who he was, raising my kids, was like having a needle stuck in my eye.

I was due at Frank and Jill's at 7. With a few hours to kill and not wanting to go back to my empty apartment, I stopped at Rocky's Sports Bar & Grill. It was end of the season and most of the players who drank at Rocky's were expected to pay off their tab before splitting for their off-season homes.

When I walked in the usual ESPN channel was instead tuned to the local news channel. The governor of Ohio, William "you can call me Bud" Hermann, had just come clean at a press conference confessing his three-year affair with the state superintendent of schools, Mary Ann Coleski. Bud's dutiful wife Collette was standing behind him looking somewhat ashen-faced.

"I've hurt my family, the voters of the state and all the other folks who looked up to me. I'm truly sorry and will spend the rest of my life trying to make amends to these people." He didn't say anything about resigning.

"Governor, who do you count among the other folks who looked up to you?" asked one reporter.

"You can call me Bud" ignored the question. Obviously, he wasn't sure who did look up to him. He promised to get counseling and would be a better person in the future.

Very few people were listening to "You can call me Bud," being just the latest in a long line of celebrities who recently have admitted to their personal failings with women, small boys, animals, alcohol, drugs, pornography and gambling.

"Hi, Stub. How's it going?' Biggie Torgelson, and previously his father, have owned Rocky's for 40 years. He placed a long-necked bottle of MGD in front of me with a glass. For whatever reason, I've never liked drinking beer out of the bottle or can. If you drink in the same place enough they know what you want. Just like in the movies I've always wanted to be able to walk into a bar and say: "Give me the usual."

Rocky's is a blue-collar bar. A shot and a beer place. Ask for a whiskey sour and they'll throw you out. Usually there are a few fans at the bar, but they leave the players alone other than a quick 'hello." I never feel like I'm going to be hassled there. Indian players had been coming to Rocky's for years.

Rocky's is a shrine to the memory of Rocky Colavito who was the hero of Cleveland in the late '50s and again in the mid-'60s when he returned to the team for a couple of years. He had matinee idol looks and real muscles, not like Jose Canseco's store-bought biceps. To Biggie, Rocky Colavito was greater than Ruth, Cobb, Wagner and Rose all rolled into one. The walls are covered with photos of Colavito in action, autographed balls and bats, a jersey as well as other uniform parts. There are some other Cleveland memorabilia from the Browns, Cavs and OSU. But Colavito dominates. It doesn't take much to get Biggie going about Rocky Colavito, 50 years after he was traded to the Tigers for Harvey Kuenn. Biggie has never gotten over it.

"Typical of the Indians. We got the biggest name in baseball and The Trader – Frank Lane, figures he needs some headlines and brings in a banjo hitter." Reminding Biggie that Kuenn was the reigning batting champion at that time never did much good.

"What was I supposed to do, call the bar Harvey's? Harvey was a big rabbit. What kind of name is that for a bar?

"Yeah. The Indians. Christ, now we got real Indians out there mulling around with shields and signs. They think we should change their name. It's politically incorrect to call a team the Indians. Bullshit. Give me a break. They've been Indians before the Indians were Indians.

"And what Indians are we talking about here? Now we go Indians with dots, not feathers?"

I had to think about that one for a minute. Biggie was just being Biggie as he walked off to take care of another customer. It wasn't long before he was back.

"Lane. The guy was a bum. That's the Indians for you. Hell, we even traded Roger Maris. The guy broke Ruth's record a few years later. Of course, he was playing for the Yankees then. It should have happened here. Nothing good ever happens in Cleveland."

Biggie went off to take care of a few other customers but soon came back. “Did you know that Colavito pitched too? Just like Ruth.”

“No. Is that right?” I knew Colavito had pitched but I didn’t want to interrupt Biggie. He was on a roll. He’s been telling the same story for 40 years. Why stop him now?

“The guy had a cannon for an arm. You can look it up. No one ever got a hit off him. He was undefeated.” Biggie was right. I had checked it out in the Baseball Encyclopedia. Colavito pitched a total of 5 innings in two games and only gave up one hit. He won one and lost none with an ERA of zero. In Biggie’s mind, Colavito was a regular arm out of the bullpen.

I once made the mistake of pointing out that Harvey Kuenn was one of the pure hitters in baseball at that time, but Biggie didn’t want to hear that. “Banjo hitter, that’s all he was. Talk about banjo hitters, we had that nutcase Piersall too. Of course, the best year he ever had was in Cleveland. Hit .322 in ’61. But, that was it. We traded him the next year. What else did he ever do other than run around the bases backward when he hit his 100th home run? He was with the Angels when he did that.”

Just for the record Colavito came back to the Indians in ’65 and had a couple more productive years though nothing like his first time around. Biggie and other Colavito fans will never forget the bitterness of the earlier trade.

“Hey, Biggie. I always wondered. What’s your real name?”

Biggie looked at me like I had asked him if he still beat his wife. His eyebrows furrowed. He looked pissed.

“What the fuck is it to you, bush leaguer?”

“Whoa. Did I hit a sore spot or what?”

“Biggie. That’s my real name?”

"Biggie? C'mon. Nobody names their kid Biggie. What's it say on your birth certificate?"

"Probably not what it says on yours, shithead." There was a long silence as we stared at each other across the bar. This was a typical exchange with Biggie. He could insult you ten different ways, but it was just Biggie being Biggie. Also, I always figured Biggie had a severe case of attention deficit disorder. He could switch conversational topics quicker than a politician running for re-election.

"Howard."

"What?"

"Howard. You heard me! It's Howard. All right? That's why I changed it to Biggie. Now get rid of the gold."

"What?"

"The gold. Get rid of it. I been meaning to tell you that since you started coming in here. It's faggot stuff. Women wear gold necklaces, not men."

"All ballplayers wear gold chains," I said. "It's a sign of our affluence."

"Yeah? Well you aren't a ballplayer anymore, are you? We put up with that shit just because you were a ballplayer. But you aren't anymore. Look around here. You see gold on any other guys? The only gold you'll find in this bunch is in their teeth. And that's only because the union health benefits paid for it. I got no patience for that crap."

"Really? I never could have guessed it."

Biggie turned soft for a minute. "Hey Stub. I'm gonna miss ya. What's the name of the kid taking your place? Fernango? Fernando? Furman. What is it?"

"Fernandez. Pedro Fernandez."

"Oh shit. One of those Dominicans. Well don't tell him about Rocky's. He wouldn't fit well in here. Tell him to hang out at Taco

Bell or wherever the spics go. Send some of the big stars around. All I get are you banjo hitters in here. That don't bring no broads or nothin.'" "Gee, Howard, there for a minute I thought you actually liked me."

Biggie ignored me. "Colavito. Now that was a star. Vic Wertz. Whatever happened to Vic Wertz? Probably got a plumbing supply store in Youngstown or something."

"I think he's dead, Biggie. Hey, it's been real. I'll stop by next time I'm in town." I shook his hand and headed for the door. I had completed my farewell at Rocky's Bar & Grill.

I stopped by the Chinaman's to pick up my laundry and then headed home. As a major league baseball player, I was a celebrity even if I wasn't the biggest star. At a laundry run by a Chinese family that didn't know baseball from opera I was just another customer. That was okay by me.

I was beginning to regret having so quickly accepted the invitation to Frank and Jill's for dinner, but I knew I couldn't back out now.

It was almost 7:30 when I got to their house in upscale Rocky River on the west side of town. The drive from Shaker Heights on the east side, post rush hour, only took about 25 minutes. Cleveland's rush hour isn't exactly gridlock to begin with. The Laportes lived in a 4-bedroom traditional style home on about a half-acre of land. As ballplayers go it was modest but that was Jill Laporte's style. She was not flashy. She was sensible and going to make sure that when Frank was through making the big bucks that they hadn't spent it all on unnecessary luxuries. I could almost guarantee that this house was paid for. No sub-prime mortgages for this gal.

She greeted me at the door with a quick hug and a kiss and held out a cold beer for me.

"I'm so glad you could make it tonight, Kenny." She never called me Stub. She was just not into nicknames. "End of another season. You have to tell us what your plans are."

Frank had the fireplace going. It felt good to offset the chill of the early fall coolness we were experiencing. "Hey, man. Nice hit today. A ribbie. A couple put outs. You had a good day all the way around."

"Frankie. I think you forget we lost 7 to 3. Just another loss in a long season. I'm glad it's over."

"That's how we feel every year this time when we don't make the playoffs. Come February and you'll be itching to get down to Arizona and get started again."

"Frankie, you seem to forget. This was it for me. I'm all done."

"Never say never, Stub. You never know. Somebody might need some veteran help next year."

Jill was busy taking care of the Laporte children, two boys and a girl between the ages of 4 and 9. They had eaten dinner earlier and she made sure they were ready for bed but were going to be allowed to stay up for a while to watch television, which in the Laporte household was limited to eight hours a week...one hour a day plus a bonus hour.

But it wasn't long before Jill called us in to dinner. The menu was a tossed salad, meatloaf, mashed potatoes and green beans, with a side of cranberry bread, baked by Jill, of course. Dessert was a two-layer cake that she had also made. It was a sensible Midwestern dinner without frills. Nothing fancy. That was Jill's way.

We talked about their family. We talked a little about Loretta and my kids over in Chicago. I assured Jill I was heading over to see them now that the season was over. We had been young baseball families together. Like Army families, baseball wives often form a bond in the absence of their husbands.

"So, Kenny, what are you going to do now?" Jill asked me.

"Well, I just want to take a little time off. I'm thinking of driving around the country to see people that I have known over the years but didn't get to spend any time with while I was playing ball. Friends. Relatives. Spend some time in the cities where we did nothing but go to a hotel and a ballpark. The only thing I ever saw in Atlanta was from the windows of the team bus. Someone told me they have the largest marine aquarium in the world there."

Frank looked at me skeptically. "Marine aquarium? Since when do you care about that?"

"I was just mentioning it as a possibility. Something to see. You ever see the movie Pulp Fiction?" I asked.

"Yeahhh?" Frank was obviously puzzled as to where this was going.

"Remember Samuel L. Jackson's role as Jules the hit man? When he decided it was time to give up the life he told Vincent he was going to walk the earth going from adventure to adventure, just like David Carradine in the old Kung Fu TV series. Well, I'm going to do the same thing except I'm going to drive rather than walk."

"Sounds to me more like a bad plot from Route 66. Who are you, Todd Stiles or Buzz Murdock?"

"Make fun of me, Frank, if you want to, but I just need to get out of here and away from baseball for a while and clear my head. This is all I have known for 16 years. I lost a marriage and family because of it. I'm not complaining. They paid us well. There are lots of mechanics, tool and die workers, and bank officers who would have traded with us in a New York minute for the opportunity to play major league baseball. But it's over for me. You got a few more years in that rubber arm of yours. You are that rarest commodity, a southpaw who never ends up on the disabled list.

"Hell, they only bring you in to pitch to one or two guys every other game or so. That's not exactly wearing you out. Teams don't even have any other guys like you in their systems. They've got young 3rd basemen at every level of the minor league organization waiting to move up every five years or so and they are bigger, stronger, and faster."

"How long will you be 'walking the earth'?" Frank asked me.

"Just like Jules told Vincent, 'until God tells me to stop.'"

"Okay, buddy. Make sure to send us a postcard."

"Do they still have postcards? I'll send you an e-mail instead."

I helped Jill clear the table and clean the dishes while Frank put the kids to bed. She told me she understood where I was in life and hoped I could find myself. She had seen a lot of ex-ballplayers over the years have readjustment problems and I know she was wondering what would happen to me.

It had been a long day, so I left early and headed home wondering which direction I would head in when I started "walking the earth," or in my case, "driving the earth."

CHAPTER 2

I slept in late the next morning. After all these years in baseball, playing night games followed by day games, followed by an overnight to the west coast and a double header the next day, I've found that I can fall asleep at almost any time I want to and wake up when I want to. I didn't have many off seasons because I played winter ball or the fall instructional league when I was younger. When I didn't I was still getting ready for the next season. Sleep was a commodity that I took when I could get it. I guess I've probably been tired for 16 years. It might be nice to have a regular sleeping schedule.

The lead story in the Metro Section of the Cleveland Plain Dealer was about a local alderman who had decided to have a sex change operation. "I have always known I was living a lie. I always knew there was a woman inside me who wanted to get out," he told the reporter. He was now planning to divorce his wife, so he could marry a man who used to be a woman tennis player. Before and after photographs of the happy couple illustrated the story better than words.

I knew that before I left town I needed to call Alexis but decided to wait until after lunch. Then I dialed her direct line at the Lakewood Sun, a suburban weekly newspaper where she was the features editor.

"This is Alexis Dudak. May I help you?" Everyone at the Sun had been trained to answer the phones the same way. "May I help you" was deemed a more welcoming phrase than "Can I help you." They had paid some consultant $10,000 to teach their employees good customer relations.

"Hey. It's Stub."

"Stub who?"

"Don't give me that. How come you weren't at the game yesterday?"

"I have a job, bush league. Not like you."

"It was my last game. I'll probably never play another game of baseball in my life."

"Probably? I think that's way too optimistic. You could drop that word and the sentence would be correct."

"Do you always have to edit all my sentences? Can't you show a little sympathy for a guy without any marketable skills going onto the job market at age 36?"

"Edit is what I do. And the word you are looking for is empathy not sympathy. Empathy from the Greek word empatheria, the projection of one's own personality into the personality of another in order to understand him better."

"I really don't need a lesson in grammar at this point. Besides, you're making all this up, right?"

"How would you know? You're a college drop out. Read "The Power of Language" by Robert Carr. Learn one new word a day and you'll be able to wow people at cocktail parties and have new boring friends."

"Alexis. Knock it off, please. I want to see you."

"I can't sleep with you anymore. I've decided it's against my journalistic ethics. Never sleep with your news sources."

"I don't see the problem. I never gave you any news."

"On the Indians there isn't any news."

"Alexis, I'm leaving town for a while."

"Good. Maybe I can save my marriage." Alexis was married to Joe Dudak, a photographer for the Cleveland Plain Dealer.

"Why would you want to do that," I asked. "Isn't it more fun this way?"

"I'm still trying to figure that out."

"How about Dolce Ristorante about 6 tonight?"

"If you're going to break up with me, why can't we go to Pizza Hut? That would make for a better story."

"I want to go to an Italian restaurant," I told her. "I feel like pasta tonight."

"Pizza Hut is an Italian restaurant. They have spaghetti on the menu, right?"

"Yes." I answered. My voice was full of sarcasm.

"And they have pizza, right?"

"Yessss."

"Spaghetti and pizza. That, an Italian restaurant, makes."

"Pizza Hut is not an Italian restaurant. They have video games there. Italian restaurants don't have video games. Goddamn it, Alexis. Why are you giving me so much shit?"

There was silence. Then I heard her voice change slightly. It sounded like she was trying not to cry.

"You're leaving me. Everyone who loves me leaves me."

"Joe hasn't left you."

"Joe doesn't love me. I don't love Joe. Joe could leave, and I really wouldn't care."

"Let's talk about this tonight. I'll see you about 6." We hung up without any other words.

I needed to get the oil changed in my 4-year-old SUV. The Jiffy Lube guys tried to sell me on changing my PCP valve, a radiator flush and new fan belt.

"No. No. No. Just change the oil." I always kept my cars in good condition so I knew I didn't need all those things. I only let the dealer mechanics touch the car in-between oil changes. There were always new guys at the Jiffy Lube each time I went there. Most of them looked like they were on a work release program.

I cancelled the newspaper delivery, filled out the card at the post office to hold my mail and called my agent. Since it looked like my career was over, I wasn't sure he would take my call. Hub Collins was an attorney by training but never liked practicing law. He admitted he wasn't a very good lawyer anyway. He was extremely overweight, seemed to have only one suit, and that usually had food stains on it.

Hub didn't have a secretary. He always answered his own phone. It's just a cell. I think he worked out of his home, his car or a coffee shop. When we met face to face it was usually at a place like Starbucks. God, I hated the coffee at Starbucks. I tried to get him to go someplace else where he could at least get free Wi-Fi, but he liked the bran muffins there.

Hub's claim to fame is he once had for a client the top player in the NBA – Eddie "The Only" Nolan, a fast-talking street player from Dallas who left a trail of destruction behind him wherever he went. He went to three colleges without ever getting past his freshman year but impressing coaches, scouts and the media wherever he went with his uncanny shooting and ball handling.

Hub got him a contract with an expansion team that would have set him up for life, as well as Hub, but "The Only" was self-destructive. He had children with 9 different women ("I don't use no raincoats when making it with my women"), was arrested twice for carrying a concealed weapon ("Lots of dudes after my bling, man."). Just about every offense the NBA could think of, "The Only" found a way to violate it: drugs, DUI, domestic battery, gambling on league games, including those that he played in.

"The Only" had difficulty with authority and moral expectations. Hub's career went the same direction as "The Only," but at least he didn't follow his client into prison. "The Only" was serving nine to 15 years at Lewisburg Federal Penitentiary for armed robbery and enough other offenses that are too many to mention.

Hub has been trying to work his way back up the ladder but the stain of "The Only" won't go away.

He answered his phone on the 2nd ring. Hub can't afford to ignore too many clients even ones like me without a future. "Hey, Stub. How ya doing, kid?"

"Hub, I thought I would let you know that I'm heading out of town for a few weeks. You can always catch me on my cell phone. Just leave a message. I might even be checking e-mail every now and then."

"Yeah, Stub. You never know if the Yankees might call and need you to bat cleanup." That was part of Hub's problem; his sense of humor was always about two steps off from everyone else. What he thought was funny was usually insensitive and personal.

I let the remark sit for about 10 seconds before replying. I know he was on the other end chuckling to himself, thinking that we were into the joke together. Here I was finishing up my mediocre career with no plans beyond tomorrow and he's making jokes about it.

"Right, Hub. Let me know when that call comes in. I'll check in with you in a few weeks." I was never sure when I didn't talk to Hub for a while whether he would still even be alive. He experienced binge bouts with drinking and depression. I could have done better when it came to a business agent. Oh well, it's too late now.

I got to Dolce Ristorante a little early and sat at the bar waiting for Alexis. She didn't show up until almost 7 p.m., an hour late. I was thinking she had stood me up, which wouldn't be all that unexpected under the circumstances.

"I was on deadline," is all she would say. No apology. No "I'm sorry." Just "I'm on deadline." Damn reporters always claim they are on deadline. They think that excuses everything. They'll be late for their own funerals because they are on deadline. The only reason I didn't leave before Alexis got there was that we had gone through this drill before.

"Did you order the pizza?" she asked me.

"Can we have a drink first? And, I don't want to have pizza."

"We should have gone to a fine Italian restaurant like Pizza Hut," she said.

I wasn't going down that path again. "Honey, please. This is our last night together for a while. Can't we enjoy each other's company without all the snide remarks?"

"Let me get this straight, bush league. Your baseball career is over. You don't have another job. You don't have a wife that I'm aware of. Your whole baseball career consisted of leaving town every two weeks. Now that you have a chance to stick around, you're leaving town again. May I ask where you are going?" Even in regular conversation Alexis would use "may" rather than "can." That money

Sun Newspapers spent on the consultant went beyond the workplace, even when she was obviously pissed at me.

"Anyplace but Cleveland."

"I've heard that ballplayers have women in every city. You're going to visit them, aren't you? I'm just your Cleveland girl. You probably have Mary in Minneapolis, Kim in Kansas City, Barbara in Boston and let's see...in Detroit it's probably Letisha."

"Letisha is a racist insinuation."

"When did you become so PC? I've heard your comments before about the Dominicans and the Jews. Don't be so holy."

"Let's move on. I'm just planning to take a trip. Okay? I need some time to cool off, think about what I want to do next. I've got to go see my kids for a few days. I want to see my sister. I haven't seen my sister in five years."

"You never told me about your sister. What's the matter with her? Why don't you see her more often?"

"I can't stand her husband."

"Why?"

"He's an asshole."

"Maybe after five years he's not an asshole anymore."

"Once an asshole, always an asshole."

"You've always been so open minded. Maybe you'll like him now."

"I'm not counting on it."

"Who else are you going to see?"

"There's this buddy of mine I played with in the minors. He's a baseball coach now at a junior college in southern Illinois. Ted Dover. We always stayed in touch. Maybe it's something I might want to do, get into college coaching."

"Don't they at least expect you to have a college degree?" Alexis said this in a tone of voice that showed her disapproval of the fact that I signed my first professional contract after my freshman year of college. That's as far as I ever got. She never let me forget it.

"Maybe. I'm not sure. I guess I'll find out. I want to drive across the U.S. and see it from the ground level. I've been flying over it all these years. I want to see what's down there."

"How far will you go?"

"Until I run into the ocean, then I'll turn around and come back."

"You probably don't even know what ocean it is."

I ignored that remark. "You know how many times I've been to LA and San Francisco without seeing anything other than a hotel room and a ballpark? I might take a ride up to Napa Valley and see the vineyards. The Redwoods. I've always wanted to see the Redwoods.

"Maybe you could fly out and meet me in San Francisco."

"Right. I'll just tell Joe I'm on assignment. Let's see, at Sun Newspapers we must get special permission to do an interview outside of Cuyahoga County. I'm sure that one will fly."

"Alexis, make something up. You've been doing it well enough for the last two years that we've been seeing each other."

"Are you coming back to Cleveland then?"

"I don't know. Do you want me to?"

"You would just come back to fuck up my marriage."

"Alexis, it's already fucked up. How much worse can I make it?"

"While you're gone Joe and I might put things back together."

"You really believe that?"

"No, but you never can tell."

Once our entrees came we ended up in harmless chit chat about the team, about Sun Newspapers, about Alexis and Joe visiting his relatives at Thanksgiving. You would have thought we were just old friends having a last dinner together. The chance of her sleeping over tonight was between slim and none.

We said our goodbyes in the parking lot. She gave me a quick kiss on the lips, nothing special, told me to drive carefully and headed off to her car. "See ya around," was all she would say.

Well, that went better than I expected, I thought to myself. With Alexis I never knew what to expect.

CHAPTER 3

I got onto I-80/90, the Ohio Turnpike, heading west. The sun was shining, just a few high cirrus clouds. Fall was in the air. When I hit the road, the temperature was about 48 degrees but the forecast called for a warm up into the low 60s.

I really wasn't sure if my first stop would be Indianapolis to see my sister or Chicago to see my kids. The latter was preferable, but the former would get that chore of out of the way and allow me to enjoy the kids when I saw them. I figured I would make my decision when I hit the junction of I-69 near Angola. Then I could shoot south if I wanted. Decision time was about three hours away.

I have satellite radio in my car, so I turned on Bloomberg News to see what was happening on Wall Street. The headline news was that Dave Kemp, CEO of America's largest steel-making firm, Kemp Steel, had announced he was gay and was leaving his wife of 32 years for his new "soul mate," Buzzy Engel, a tattoo artist and former Iditarod Sled Race winner. Kemp Steel's stock price had dropped 14 per cent and the SEC was planning to step in and stop trading. The Kemp Steel board of directors had asked for Kemp's resignation but so far, he had refused, saying that he wanted to show America that a 64-year-old homosexual executive could effectively run a major corporation. He felt that his sexual identity had nothing to do with his leadership abilities.

"For the first time in my life I feel totally free," he said in an interview with a Bloomberg reporter. "I now can run the business without the stress of my secret personal life hanging over me."

My first stop was at an Ohio Turnpike rest plaza west of Toledo. These places used to be pit stops, run down, dingy. Most of them had one restaurant choice run by a company like Howard Johnson with a lot of angry people behind the counter.

I had to give someone credit for rethinking the business model. I can't help but think that run right, you must be able to make money. After all, it's not like people have a lot of other choices on a controlled access highway. Today these plazas feature food courts; true it's fast food, but that's exactly what travelers want. Pee, eat and go. All I wanted was a cup of coffee. I always check out the large map on the wall that has a little icon that says: "YOU ARE HERE." It makes me feel good to know where I am, although I've always been a bit of a map freak so it's not that I don't know in the first place.

I'm a bit of a snob when it comes to people who don't have the same sense of direction I do. I keep hearing them talk about their GPS and how they don't go anyplace without it. I've been driving for 20 years now and it seems that a combination of maps, road signs and my own intuition get me where I want to go without too much problem.

As I crossed into Indiana under the big sign that proclaimed the Hoosier State "The Crossroads of America," I made up my mind to head to Indianapolis. One night with my sister Tina, her asshole husband Bob and their kids and I could check that off my list.

Tina had issued the invite a few weeks ago via e-mail when she had heard that I was going to retire. I love my sister and have always been close to her even though she married Bob. I had stayed a bit vague on my exact travel plans but that was fine with her. She said they had nothing planned and that I should come down to see them whenever.

I would have preferred to stay in a hotel and I know Bob would have wanted me there also. That's the reason I decided to take Tina's invite to stay in the boys' room, just to annoy Bob. They have three kids, two boys, Justin, 9, and "little" Bob, 7, and a daughter Sylvia, 3.

As I passed the exits for Fort Wayne I remembered when Loretta and I were married, and we took a Caribbean cruise during the offseason. Loretta got a virus and spent most of the cruise throwing up in our cabin. I spent most of my time wandering the ship by myself including time in the library where among the limited collection was an autobiography written by Dave Thomas, founder of the Wendy Hamburger chain. I thought of him because he was from Fort Wayne, where he learned the business working in a local chicken restaurant before moving onto work for The Colonel at Kentucky Fried Chicken.

As a vanity book goes, it wasn't a half bad read. I admire entrepreneurs. Thomas was an orphan who first learned how to cook while serving in the Army. He passed away a few years ago but he always appeared in commercials for his restaurant chain and I remember that he seemed like a good guy. He was an American success story.

About the time I passed Marion, I called Tina on my cell phone and left a message on her machine that I would be arriving later that afternoon, staying the night and leaving the next day.

"I'm really looking forward to seeing you and the kids." Tina knew Bob and I didn't like each other so I didn't bother at any pretense about wanting to see Bob. But, I knew he came with the package. He tolerated me for the same reason.

So, what's my problem with Bob? He's a schemer. He has more schemes than Ralph Kramden. There's always another deal he has going that's worth millions. Or so he says. He's also a conspiracy nut. He watches Fox News non-stop. His opinions come directly from the mouths of Sean Hannity and Rush Limbaugh.

When you try to disagree with him about anything, he's one of those guys who always challenges you with a bet. His hand shoots out for a shake as he says: "Ten bucks that I'm right. Ten bucks. C'mon. Put your money where your mouth is." What pisses me off most is that he's usually right, so I've learned to just avoid any confrontation.

Bob works in shopping mall development. They belong to a country club, their credit cards are maxed out, and the mortgage on their big house in suburban Carmel eats up most of their monthly income. From the outside, Bob gives the appearance of wealth. Inside, the house is furnished by IKEA. Bob is always one step away from financial bankruptcy, a condition which he has experienced, or to listen to him, one step away from being the next Warren Buffet. At least he sees the glass as being half full rather than half empty. I have to give him that.

When his schemes don't work out, he blames it on the damn liberals, and the "international Jewish conspiracy."

I've always felt that Bob is envious of my major league career, as mediocre as it might have been. Justin and "little" Bob glory in the fact that their uncle is a professional baseball player. They have my baseball cards and posters decorating the room. I like it because I'm sure it rankles "big" Bob every time he goes into their room to see a big picture of me on the wall.

I played for the Indianapolis Indians for one year in Triple-A. It's a nice town. I never mind getting back there. There are some good restaurants and lots of things to do. I needed to kill a couple hours before going to Tina's house, so I took a ride around the city, checking out all the new athletic facilities. Indianapolis remade itself in the '70s and '80s into a center for amateur athletics. They also built a new state-of-the-art stadium for the Indians downtown which I wanted to see.

When I played there we were in old Bush Stadium on the west side of town. It was used for filming "Eight Men Out," which was about baseball in 1919. Bush Stadium fit the mold of the times. They used it for a few years for midget car racing, but that didn't work out so well. So now it just sits there waiting for a new plan. It will probably end up being knocked down and my brother-in-law will try to build a strip mall there.

Ballplayers have sentimental feelings about stadiums, particularly when they had some success there. I had a good season in Indianapolis and will always remember the winning home run I hit in the bottom of the 13th inning to beat the Rochester Red Wings to give us the pennant that year. It's the minor leagues where we are competing as much against our own teammates to move up as well as the other clubs. But there's still that competitiveness and team spirit that we were all raised with and it comes out at times like that.

It was almost 6 p.m. when I got to Tina's. My timing was calculated on having to spend the least amount of time with Bob and arriving at cocktail hour would help us overcome the social tension. I was pleased when I got there to discover Bob was at a business meeting and would be late, so I got to spend some quality time with Tina and the kids before Bigmouth Bob showed up.

Tina fed the kids while she and I talked. We exchanged small talk about her kids and her activities. I told her what I knew about Loretta and my kids in Chicago and let her know I was headed there next. Tina and Loretta always seemed to like each other. Our divorce came as a surprise to the whole family and Loretta continued to exchange Christmas cards with my family.

"So, what are you going to do next, Stub?"

"I don't really know. I'm just going to walk the earth for a while."

"What?"

"Nothing. Just an expression that covers my activities for the short term. I'll worry about it when I get back. Then I can figure out what to do."

"Can you get a coaching job or stay in baseball somehow?"

"Probably, but the life of a baseball lifer never really appealed to me. But, then again, you never say never."

The kids were allowed to stay up and watch a couple TV shows. Tina got tired of waiting for Bob, so we started to eat dinner without him. About the time I got done with my salad, Bob came through the front door, much too soon for me.

"Hey, bush league! How's it going?"

"Good, Bob. Thanks for your thoughtful inquiry." There were a couple times in our relationship that I had referred to Bob as "Chapter 11" but I knew that was upsetting to Tina, so I let it go.

"Sorry I'm late, honey," he said to Tina. "We've got another deal cooking. I couldn't get out of the office."

This was obviously not the first time Bob was late for dinner due to a hot deal. My suspicion is that he was playing solitaire on his computer and just didn't want to see me any more than I wanted to see him.

In respect to Tina, Bob and I had always tried to keep the tension between us to a minimum. I was sure this night would proceed the same way.

"So, what are you going to do now that you've hung up the spikes?"

"I'm going to walk the earth."

"Huh?"

"I'm just taking some time to go see some people that I know around the country and then I'll make up my mind. I've got a few offers on the table."

"Real estate, sport. That's where it's always been, and it always will be. We got so many projects going these days I can't keep my head on straight."

"Tell me about it, Bob."

He didn't expect that and like I figured, he would find a way not to tell me. "Can't do it. Confidential. But some of them are really big."

So, the night went, lots of small talk, lots of evasion of specifics on both sides of the table. Tina would fill in the silent moments with a story about the kids, or her activity at their church where she worked 20 hours a week as the assistant to the pastor. All in all, it was an uneventful life consumed by the love she had for her children and her tolerance of their father.

After dessert we went into the den to watch some TV. Bob was constantly checking his iPhone, texting or e-mailing messages back and forth, mumbling to himself about the content. His phone rang three or four times and he would leave the room to have animated conversations. Tina never seemed to show any signs of happiness. She would occasionally look at me and roll her eyes slightly when Bob would get another call or text message.

Finally, I excused myself and said I was going to turn in early. Great dinner. Enjoyed getting caught up but it had been a long day and I'll see you in the morning. Part of it was true. Part of it was just having had enough of Bob and figuring he might be gone in the morning when I got up and I wouldn't have to see him again. That's just how it happened.

Tina got the boys off to school and her daughter to pre-school. We met for breakfast at the Denny's six blocks from their house. Nothing like the Grand Slam Breakfast to start the day.

"I wish you could stay a bit longer. The kids always enjoy having you here. Justin and Bobby have all your baseball cards and know all your statistics. Their uncle the baseball player."

"And, of course, Bob enjoys having me around as well, right?"

"You just have to ignore him."

"You mean like you've done for the past 12 years?"

She didn't say anything for a while. I thought maybe I had gone too far with my remarks.

"I'm really not sure what Bob does at work. He's gone a lot. He never tells me how much money we have or what he gets paid. I've never met anyone at his job. I don't even really know who he works for or where he goes to work. He doesn't tell me anything. He just gets lots of phone calls, e-mails and text messages. He pretty much ignores me and the kids. This isn't easy, Stub."

"Have you talked with anyone, Tina? A counselor? What about the pastor? You work with him at the church. Couldn't you get some advice from him?"

"He's a she. And, yes, I have talked with her a little bit about our situation, but I'm just not ready to get into it too deeply. I've just learned to keep my mouth shut and take care of my kids.

"I've never really asked you about what happened with you and Loretta. Why and how did you guys decide to go in opposite directions? That seems to have worked out okay for you."

"I guess you could put it that way if you figure I only see my kids a few times a year. But that's more due to being a baseball player. Most of the guys who are married only seem to see their kids a few times a year. You pay a price with your family for the big bucks.

"I don't know. We just sort of grew apart. You know all those stories about professional athletes fooling around on the road. Well, some of them are true. Some aren't. For the first few years of our marriage I didn't mess around. You don't have a lot of time. You are at the ballpark or back in the hotel sleeping. Where guys get in trouble is when they head to the clubs after a night game. There are always the 'Annies' around.

"When the season was over I would try to be a good husband and father. Of course, there were a couple of years the club wanted me to play winter ball so that was just more time away. We never could have a real family life.

"There was no one moment that brought the marriage to an end. Loretta is an independent person and she found other things to do with her life other than wait around for me. It was one of those things where we both knew. A lot of baseball marriages end that way. There isn't any real animosity. I'm thankful for that."

We both fell silent for a couple of minutes, caught up in our own thoughts. “If you ever decide to leave him, let me know. Wherever I’m at I’ll find a way to get here and help you out. Make sure to call me first. Don’t just go off on your own.”

I knew she was on the edge of tears. Her eyes met mine and she nodded whispering, “Thanks. I love you.”

CHAPTER

4

My car was packed. I hit the road right from the restaurant. We were only 5 minutes from I-465, the interstate that circles Indianapolis. Ten minutes later I was headed north on I-65 flowing into the heavy truck traffic that made this otherwise boring drive an adventure. Chicago was three hours away.

I passed Lafayette and the signs for Tippecanoe, the battlefield made famous by Indiana's first son, President William Henry Harrison. "Tippecanoe and Tyler Too." I remembered that from my eighth-grade history class. I had always told myself that when I had the time, like now, I would stop to visit battlefields and read historical markers. Easier said than done. I was rolling along at 75 mph and this detour would have taken at least an hour or more. I wasn't up for it. I'll do it another time, I told myself, knowing that I probably wouldn't.

I wanted to get to Chicago before the afternoon rush hour, which in my experience seemed to get earlier all the time. It used to be that

4:30 p.m. was when the traffic got to be a bitch. My last few times in town, I wasn't sure when rush hour started or ended. It just seemed like endless stop and go traffic. But, I figured that an early afternoon arrival still made things easier.

Loretta lived in Naperville, in the far western suburbs, which made things even easier. I checked into the local Fairfield Inn. It's run by Marriott. In baseball we stayed in a lot of Marriott hotels, so I had gotten into their "frequent stay" plan and had built up thousands of points which I guess entitled me to free nights and discounts throughout their chain. The problem was that I never seemed to cash in. I would occasionally go on-line to check my account but then could never figure out how or where to use the points. It was one of the goals I had in retirement, to figure out how to use some of this stuff.

Loretta worked in human resources for a local computer firm. She and I rarely talked on the phone anymore. It was all e-mail. I had let her know when I would be in town. She said we should have dinner that night and she had arranged for me to spend the next three days with the kids. She always had a good sense of how these things should go.

To her credit, or maybe our credit, this divorce thing had worked out okay. She had set up a Facebook account for the kids so that I could check in on them and their activities. We weren't like other divorced couples, there was no haggling. I did what I could as an absentee father. There was never any problem with my child support payments. We had set it up with the ballclub for a direct deposit to Loretta's account. Of course, now we would have to figure something else out, but I didn't have to worry about money for a while. Loretta would still get the money on time. I guessed it was one of the things we would discuss tonight.

She worked as a human resources manager for a local computer software company. We had agreed to meet at Morton's, one of your overpriced steak joints that were struggling in this economy. Who needs a $52 steak with an ala carte $12 salad, $6 baked potato, and $8 serving of 3 asparagus spears? I knew this meal, plus a bottle of wine would set me back a couple hundred bucks at least, but since this was the mother of my children and I didn't see her that often I thought it would be a treat for her.

Most normal people couldn't afford to eat there, and corporate expense accounts were under attack everywhere. Plus, it being a normally slow Wednesday night I figured it would be quiet. We could hear ourselves talk. I was looking forward to seeing her. I had never stopped loving her. We just had grown tired of our life together.

I had made reservations for 7 p.m. Loretta wanted to be able to leave work at 5 p.m., pick up the kids from school, take them home and get dinner on the table for them before the sitter showed up. Scotty was in 2nd grade. Nicole was in all-day kindergarten.

I arrived at the restaurant early and sat at the bar. I ordered a Guinness. This is one of those great drinking secrets that most people don't know. Guinness looks and sounds lethal, but since it doesn't have any carbonation it doesn't make you fuzzy. And, the alcohol content is more akin to a light beer with some actual taste.

She was right on time looking gorgeous as always. Loretta is tall, about 5'9", auburn hair and green eyes. She always was a knockout. Plus, she is a great mother and was always good at every job. I always wondered how I screwed up this relationship. Every time I saw her I hoped we could get together again.

We kissed, hugged and told each other how good we looked. We had the hostess seat us. She ordered a glass of chardonnay. I asked how the kids were and if they were ready for some daddy-time. All the usual chit chat of a couple who were once in love, probably still are at some level, but now made the best of a past relationship because of the children, innocent victims of our inability to get along.

Then she dropped the bomb.

"Stub, I need to tell you something. I'm getting married."

I heard her but then again, I didn't hear her. I didn't want to hear what I had heard. I was feeling so many emotions at that time that I wasn't sure which one mattered. I was still in love with Loretta. I still considered her my wife. I didn't want my kids to be raised by another man. I was unemployed for the first time in my life and feeling somewhat lost.

I knew the Alexis thing was just that, the Alexis thing. This wasn't unexpected news. But, when I finally heard it, well, it was unexpected.

"When?" That was all I could say.

"New Year's Eve. We decided it would be fun to start off the New Year as a married couple." She smiled when she told me. I think she wanted me to be part of her excitement. I was having a difficult time doing that.

"Yeah. Well, Happy New Year. What do the kids think about this?"

"They know. They understand. They like Bill. He's been great to them."

I really didn't want to hear that. I was hoping he would be a son-of-a-bitch so that I could rescue them and Loretta. But, I also knew that Loretta would never marry a son-of-a-bitch, unless of course I fit into that category.

She insisted on telling me about Bill Warski even though I didn't want to hear about him. "You need to listen. He's going to be spending a lot more time with your children then you are."

Oooh. Shot in the stomach on that one.

"Thanks. I really needed that," I answered sarcastically.

Bill was widowed. His wife died of breast cancer six years ago. He had two children, older than ours. Both were in high school. This would be a blended family for a few years until his kids left for college. He was nine years older than Loretta, but that figured. She was always at least nine years older than me maturity-wise so someone of that age differential would fit her well. He had a law enforcement degree from a local university and had served as a police officer for 11 years before taking the job as head of security at the Argonne National Laboratory in suburban Chicago.

This wasn't even a guy whose ass I thought I could kick. Why couldn't she be marrying some weenie who was a tax accountant?

Loretta and I had handled the divorce and the after years a lot better than most people. There was never a question about who was better equipped to raise the children. I knew she would eventually get married and it would be to a quality person. From everything she told me I knew Bill would be a likeable guy, I just didn't want to like him.

We finally got around to me.

"So, what are you going to do now?"

"I was afraid you were going to ask me that question," I said. She laughed.

I told her about just taking some time to drive around the country and see people. I had enough money socked away that I could take the time and figure out what I should do next. I didn't use the line about "walking the earth." Particularly now that she was marrying a law enforcement professional, I thought that sounded a bit wacky.

"Have you thought about moving back to Chicago to be closer to the kids?" She wanted to know for more reasons than one.

"Yes. Of course. But right now, after what I just heard, maybe it's best that I just stay away for a while."

"That's up to you. Are you seeing anyone?"

"Sort of." I really didn't want to go there. I couldn't explain my relationship to Alexis to myself, much less have Loretta understand. She would just see it for what it was, a baseball industry fling. She had seen it before although I had always been faithful during our marriage. It was my teammates that she had witnessed over and over again.

We spent the rest of the dinner just trying to get through it. There were a few minutes when I digressed into a bit of self-pity, commenting about how I had screwed up our marriage. It was entirely my fault, I commented.

Loretta did what she always did and assured me that I was a good father and had been a good husband. We just had other issues and baseball was not conducive to our family's wellbeing. This was all old ground but occasionally necessary to review. As divorced couples go, we had handled it all fairly well.

The rest of the night we stayed on safe ground and talked about the kids' activities. I asked if I could come by in the morning and take them to school. Then I would pick them up afterwards. She thought that was all a good idea.

Tomorrow was Thursday. They had a three-day weekend coming up as Friday was a teacher conference day. I had agreed to take the kids through Sunday. The problem was that I hadn't thought this through very well and I wasn't quite sure where we would go or what we would do. I thought I would figure it out while they were in school. To my surprise, Loretta didn't question me about my plans, though I knew I would have to give her a detailed schedule or she wouldn't let them go. I had 24 hours to come up with a plan.

We said good night and headed off in our respective directions. She went home. I went to a local bar. I didn't feel like driving downtown and the western suburbs had lots of watering holes. There is a large singles, doubles, and triples community to put it in baseball terms, all trying to hit home runs. I know that sounds corny, but how better to explain a lot of people on the prowl in these trendy sports bars and grills.

It's a habit that I developed from having been on the road half the year my entire adult life, but whenever I'm in a bar I can't help but to survey the crowd to see who I might end up sleeping with that night. As a minor sports celebrity I've had many opportunities. I didn't think this was a night that I would work too hard to make that happen.

I sort of watched an early season NBA game on one of the big screens while I nursed a beer. I'm not even sure who was playing, a couple of west coast teams I think. My mind was mostly on Loretta...and Bill. I put a face on him. I figured as an ex-cop and present security chief he was probably ugly. Cops are always ugly.

I went back to the hotel early and tried to sleep but it wasn't easy. I had the alarm set for 6 a.m. I always eat breakfast, the most important meal of the day. I wanted to get to Loretta's house to pick up the kids by 7:30 a.m. They needed to be to their respective schools no later than 8 a.m.

I woke up with that buzz that comes without having enough sleep. A few cups of coffee and I would be good until early afternoon. When you stay at a hotel you always must try to figure out when the room maid would be through cleaning. Then I could come back and take a nap.

In the breakfast room of the Fairfield Inn it always seems like there's at least one person talking loudly on a cell phone. You just don't need that in the morning. This time it was a skinny guy with a long nose who was trying to explain to corporate why his appointment with his big client had not gone well. The best I could understand was that they were talking to another vendor and big nose wasn't sure what to do about it. That was his problem, not mine. I tried to eat my bagel and watch the morning news broadcast. Spreading cream cheese with one of those plastic knives they have there is always a challenge. That added to my annoyance.

Loretta's house was a split-level ranch built in the late '70s. It was in a well-kept older subdivision on the east side of town. Everything in Naperville seems "well kept." We had bought the house seven years ago. It was never even a question during the divorce proceedings that she would get to keep it. Who knew where I was going to be and, as we discovered, eventually that was Cleveland.

I noticed that the outside woodwork had been painted recently. I was never mister handyman, but I had successfully replaced a gutter and downspout on one side of the house and I couldn't help but take a quick look to see how it was faring. I was proud to see that it looked like it was still doing the job.

I had to be on a ladder to do that work. Professional athletes are constantly warned by our teams and our agents to not do those sorts of things. Most of us are not exactly handy and falling off ladders was a quick way to end your career. That was foremost on my mind and probably contributed to my being extra cautious.

I wasn't exactly sure how the kids were going to react to me. I hadn't seen them since August, which was the last time we were in town to play the White Sox. I suppose all divorced parents who are separated from their kids always wonder if they will even remember them the next time they are together. Kids of that age have a lot of other things to occupy their minds. You always fear that as an absent parent you will probably rank somewhere down below Sponge Bob Square Pants.

It turns out that I worried unnecessarily. Both kids screamed out "Daddy" when they saw me. We had lots of hugs and kisses. Loretta watched with a smile. She had never gotten into this "dump on Daddy" thing that a lot of divorced parents did. I knew she would never do that and it made me even more committed to be a good divorced father and ex-husband.

The kids were like pent-up puppies trying to tell me about all the things they were doing and about their friends and schools. I let them ramble and responded with lots of "that's great sweetie," type answers. Nicole gave me more hugs and kisses as I dropped her off at her school, but I figure Scotty didn't want his friends see him hugging his dad, so he just said "goodbye, I'll see you later."

Fortunately, they never asked me what we were going to do this weekend.

I put in a call to Lee Crossland, a sports writer for the Chicago Tribune. I had gotten to know Lee when I played for the White Sox. He was up for lunch. I headed downtown.

Listening to the radio while navigating the eternal traffic jams on the Eisenhower Expressway, the lead story was about a U.S. Senator from Massachusetts getting caught in a hooker sting in south Boston. Well, he thought it was a hooker. Turned out it was an undercover policewoman. The senator claimed he was just doing some original street research for a bill he wanted to introduce in the Senate to create vocational training for sex industry workers. He assured his constituency that he had no intention of having sex with this woman. He claimed that his offer to pay her was just for her time, so they could have a discussion. He was going to take notes and get her opinions on how his bill would be most effective.

Yes, he did plan to get a receipt from her and submit it as part of his office expenses paid for by taxpayers. His attorney assured the public that the real story would eventually come out and accused the police of grandstanding trying to make his client look bad in retribution for his support of law enforcement budget cuts.

I parked my car in the Loop. I knew it was going to be a minimum of $40 but that's the cost of living in a big city.

There are lots of new trendy restaurants in the River North area of Chicago. But Lee wasn't into trendy, so he suggested we meet at Andy's, a favorite dive of his for as long as he has been in the newspaper industry, which sometimes seemed to pre-date Gutenberg.

Lee was at the bar drinking coffee when I arrived. No one drank on their lunch hour anymore. Lee had been a drinker and a smoker. Newspaper people are famous for keeping piles of old newspapers on their desk just in case they need to look up something that was previously published.

Lee wasn't the first reporter to get drunk and set fire to his desk from careless smoking habits. But he was one of the last because newsrooms were a changing environment. People with drinking problems were told to get help or find another job. Smokers enjoying their habits stood on a small piece of cement outside the building shivering in the dead of winter to get in those few precious puffs. Editors no longer had patience for absent reporters who were on another smoking break.

"Hey, Stub. Good to see you man." We shook hands and told each other how good we looked.

"Great to see you."

"It's been too long."

I suppose we could have gone on like that for a while, but we were both hungry. Andy's usually began to fill up by 12:30. We were there early so we had our choice of seating arrangements. We took a booth along the wall. We weren't exactly celebrities, but both of us had been in the newspaper often enough that we could be recognized. Andy also was a semi-regular on the Tribune's cable TV show called "The Sportswriters." He would occasionally get hassled by fans who disagreed with his opinions.

"Every week some knucklehead calls in to complain that the Sox, the Cubs, the Bulls, take your pick, are cheap and just don't want to pay for good players," Lee said. "It's always the same complaint, cheap, cheap, cheap. This is usually from some guy who works the overnight shift at the mill and drives a 12-year-old car."

"Yeah, well I can buy into that. I've had a little experience with it, you know."

"Hey, remember what Bill Veeck said one time, 'It wasn't the cost of stardom that bothered him, it was the cost of mediocrity.'"

"In other words, you're telling me I was mediocre. Right?"

"A .268 lifetime batting average? Do I need to say more? Not exactly Hall of Fame credentials."

"Thanks, Lee. For that remark you can buy lunch."

"It's on me, buddy. I still have a job, although I'm not sure for how much longer."

The newspaper industry had been in a major meltdown for several years now. The Tribune Company, which owned numerous other newspapers and media outlets, had been taken private from being a public company and was having trouble making its debt service. Huge cuts were taking place throughout the organization and veteran reporters like Lee never knew exactly when the ax would fall on them. A hard charging young reporter from Appleton or Peoria would gladly come to Chicago for about half what Lee was making.

"So, do you have a job? What are you going to do?" He asked me the same question everyone asks me.

"Not yet. I need to take a little time and think about it. I've got some money socked away."

"Don't take too long. The time flies and the longer you're on the beach the harder it is to find something. You're what, 36? You don't have a resume. What can you do?"

"You're not the first person to make that point to me. I don't like to dwell on it too long or I get depressed. What's going on with your job?"

"Same old, same old. The jocks keep getting younger. I keep getting older. The newspaper continues to get more irrelevant. People keep leaving for these Internet gigs. It's not the same as it used to be. I'm just trying to hang on for a couple more years."

We ordered lunch. I had a club sandwich with fries on the side. Lee had the quiche of the day. "Real men are not afraid to eat quiche," he commented. That has become one of the most overused jokes between men who like quiche.

Common ground for us was sports, particularly baseball, of course. Lee had been a beat reporter for both the Cubs and the White Sox at one time or another. He didn't hide his loyalties. He grew up in Calumet City, a blue-collar southern suburb that was the heart of Sox territory. He knew that Sox players suffered a slight inferiority complex because since the '80s the Cubs had become the favorite team in the city. It wasn't always like that. In earlier years the Sox used to always outdraw the Cubs, but various ownerships had made mistakes along the way.

The management and mismanagement of the professional sports franchises in Chicago were candidates for Harvard Business School case studies.

Traditionally, when the Sox are out of town the Cubs are at home and vice versa. But occasionally there is a quirk in the schedule and we would end up playing at home on the same day. Inevitably the Cubs attendance would always outdraw us by several thousand even though we had the new ballpark, easier access and more parking. But going to ancient Wrigley Field was a happening. They drew well whether they were having a good year or a bad year. The Sox only draw well when they are winning.

We talked about baseball, about the newspaper industry, about his family, which was somewhat dysfunctional, and about my family. We were just getting caught up on the news with an old friend. I didn't have any other agenda nor did he.

There are two common relationships between professional athletes and sportswriters. There are the jocks that don't trust any reporters. They are guarded in their comments and would never allow a reporter to be a friend. Trust is not a word that applies.

Then there is the suck-up. This is usually the guy who wants to be a broadcaster or front office type when it's all over. He's always available for a quote, a pun, or the anonymous leak.

With Lee and me it was neither. We had formed an easy friendship. He's quite a few years older than me. But, back when he was covering the Sox and we would be on the road we found ourselves spending time together at dinner in the hotel or an occasional drink at the bar. I never had to worry with him about what was on or off the record. He just seemed to have a good sense of that. We found we had a lot in common. We read the same types of books, we both enjoyed fishing and we played golf together. He and his wife had been to our house for dinner when Loretta and I were still married. When I was with the Indians and we played in Chicago he invited me to his house, although, due to his strained marriage it wasn't exactly fun.

Lee's two grown children were having difficulties in their lives.

His daughter was estranged from them. Last they heard she was part of the homeless community in San Francisco and had been in and out of rehab. His son had joined the Army, which Lee thought was a good move for a kid who was seemingly a bit lost in life, until he pulled a disappearing act during basic training and was eventually declared a deserter. He had now been on the lam for two years and was on an FBI watch list.

I must admit that the only real bumps in the road I have had in my life are the divorce from Loretta which could have been much worse and an occasional batting slump that might have reached eight hitless games. There is no feeling sorry for myself. I look at Lee and think how each day he must feel like a real failure as a parent. He probably never has a really good day thinking about his kids. My kids are still young. I don't know what Loretta and I have to face in the future. Some days it scares the hell out of me thinking about it. I just hope we do the right things, so we don't have to feel the pain that Lee Crossland and his wife must feel.

After lunch I headed back out to the suburbs. The trick in getting out of Chicago in late afternoon is to hit the expressways before 3 p.m. Traffic on the Eisenhower going west was muddled, a bit stop and go, but I made it back to Naperville in 45 minutes, which is more than satisfactory.

I made the rounds to the kids' schools. Nicole was excited about our spending the next three days together. Scotty seemed to have a few other things on his mind. He was at that age where he had more friends and things to do. He did seem to enjoy the attention that he got from his buddies about being the son of a major league baseball player. That part of this relationship was okay with him. But, he wasn't sure that he wanted to give up an entire weekend to spend with his little sister and his absentee father.

We went to dinner at the local Portillo's Restaurant where hot dogs and fries were the main menu item. What kid doesn't like hot dogs?

"What do you guys think of Bill, your mom's friend?" I wasn't sure it was good politics to ask but I am their father. I needed to know about this guy if he was to become their substitute father.

"Bill has a really neat car," Nicole told me. "I like to ride in it."

"Oh? Tell me about it." For a moment I forgot she was 5. You can't have a normal conversation with a five-year-old. That being said, she did pretty good in explaining that it was a bright red color, which she liked, and that it didn't have a top.

"Ah. A convertible," I explained. She kept right on telling me how windy it was and how her mother made her wear a heavy jacket every time she rode with Bill.

Scotty said that Bill had taken them to some cool places like the zoo and the museum and down to the lakefront to see the fireworks on the Fourth of July. He also liked Bill's kids.

The night went well. I was pleased. We just seemed to get back into the father and kids role. I just wasn't sure what to expect.

When we returned to Loretta's house, Bill was there. We shook hands. I figured he was probably as nervous as I was. The kids went into the TV room, leaving the adults to our own mischief.

We all engaged in polite small talk about the kids, about our activities. Bill was complimentary about my playing career, saying he had watched me many times, particularly when I played for the Sox. Of course, everyone says that to your face. They never tell you that they booed you after an error or a strikeout. There are a lot of wackos at ball parks. I have yet to meet one who admits to it. One year we were playing the Royals at home when a couple of drunk guys jumped out of the stands and ran over to attack the Royals' first base coach. Turned out they were a father and son. They both ended up getting jail time.

Bill asked me what I thought about him and Loretta getting married and his involvement with Scott and Nicole. I had to admit that he had balls. But, then again, he's a cop, so I guess I must figure him for being an upfront sort of guy. I hated to admit that I liked him, but I figured if someone was going to be raising my kids besides myself this guy seemed like a good choice.

What could I say? "Hey, mess with my kids and I'll beat the shit out of you?" That probably wasn't going to go over well. Plus, I didn't think I could beat the shit out of him. He had that look about him that said he could pistol whip me to death.

I had accepted a long time ago that there was going to be some other father figure in their lives other than me. I sucked it up and wished them both well and promised that I would not be a pain-in-the-ass absentee father.

"I'm not really sure what I'm going to do next. That's why I want to take this trip," I told them. "Hopefully, I can put a few things together."

The subject that I knew was on Loretta's mind was wondering how much money I did have socked away. I had never missed a child support payment. It was always taken directly out of my paycheck and sent to her. But now that I didn't have a paycheck she had to be wondering about my financial situation. Everyone assumed that baseball players made a lot of money, and comparatively speaking during our careers, that's true. But, when the money train ends, it ends. I was 36 years old without a resume to do anything outside of baseball.

Unlike a lot of other players, I had been careful with my money. I didn't have children out of wedlock to support. I hadn't spent money on flashy jewelry. I had always driven sensible cars. My housing was distinctly middle class. I hadn't given my money to some shylock to invest in oil wells. I may not have been a college graduate, but I had enough sense to understand basic financial management. My parents had been children of the Depression and were always frugal. Those traits were passed on to me.

Loretta knew what my total assets and pay were like when we divorced. But that was four years ago. I didn't have to tell her now unless the support payments became an issue.

I waited for her to broach the subject.

"Stub, I do have to ask you how you intend to make your child support payments now that you're not employed." That sentence hung in the air like a fart in church.

So far, we had all been handling this like adults without any major tension. I could have told her that I had already made arrangements for a direct payment from my bank account but just out of spite I decided to let her wonder.

"Don't worry. You'll get the money, just like you always have."

"Can I ask how this will happen?"

"You can ask, but I don't think it matters. It'll be taken care of." I could see she didn't appreciate the evasion and she was about to respond and cite her right to know. Bill was sitting next to her on the couch and could see it coming also. It was obvious he had been married before and knew that this was a subject best left until and when it became a problem.

"Honey, I think if Stub says he has made arrangements, then I think that's all we need to know now." Bill got the same look that I used to get when I said something Loretta didn't like.

I thought "Good luck, Bill. Better you than me."

CHAPTER 5

Saturday morning, I picked the kids up early. Since Bill and Loretta had taken them to all the usual spots in Chicago I decided I would show them Milwaukee. It's just 90 miles north on the toll way, assuming road construction is at a minimum. They have a good zoo up there with a particularly ferocious looking gorilla named Samson who bellows and entertains people from behind a solid glass shield.

Plus, there are some pretty good German restaurants. I knew that was more of a draw for me than it was for the kids. They would probably prefer hamburgers, but this was what divorced fathers did, they spend money on things the kids would never appreciate in the hopes that it would make them feel better.

To an adult it's a short ride up there. I didn't know how the kids would react. It still was going to be three hours in the car up and back. I had heard from other divorced fathers how awful some of these weekends with their kids could be. The kids resent being taken away from their homes and their friends to satisfy a court order that they spend quality time with a father who they hardly ever see.

I wondered if Loretta would be concerned that I was taking them across the state line, but we still had enough mutual trust that she didn't figure that Milwaukee would exactly equate with an estranged father taking his kids to Brazil.

It just so happened that I do know a woman in Milwaukee who was worth a phone call. Jennifer Block was living in Cleveland when I met her. She moved to Milwaukee a year ago to take a job with Wells Fargo Bank. She was 29 and on the fast management track. Maybe Alexis was right about having a girlfriend in every city. Although Milwaukee is in the National League the only time I played there were a couple of inter-league games. I gave her a call before leaving Chicago to see if she could meet us.

"What do you think, I have nothing else to do but wait around for you to call me? I do have a social life you know."

"I understand. I was just hoping that I might catch you on an open weekend. It's been awhile since we saw each other," I said.

"No shit. It's been more like a year since I left Cleveland. Thanks for all the phone calls and letters."

"People don't write letters anymore."

"Fine. What about an e-mail occasionally?" I ignored the comment. I was pretty sure I had e-mailed her a few times and I think she never responded.

"You're bringing your kids? I don't know much about kids. You are aware of that. Right?"

"Just be nice to them. They're human beings. It's just for a few hours. I have to take them back to Chicago tonight. You could go to the zoo with us and then we can have dinner and get caught up."

"I have a job, you know."

"Are you working on Saturday?"

"Of course, I'm working on Saturday. We all work on Saturday. Haven't you heard what's going on in the banking industry? We are all overpaid evildoers. We work on Saturday so we can screw the public six days a week. We rest on the Sabbath." She waited for a reaction but didn't get one from me. "Okay. I'll leave at noon. Meet me at Del Debbio's on Plankinton Avenue downtown for lunch then we can go to the zoo. I can hardly wait."

It seemed like almost everyone I knew these days was under a lot of pressure from one direction or another. They owed too much money on their house, they were in danger of losing their job, and taxes were too high, medical care was sketchy at the best. The U.S. couldn't get out of the wars that we started following 9/11. The world seemed to be in a mess.

I had bought a new iPhone about a week before I left Cleveland, but I needed a seminar to learn how to use it. In my spare time I had been playing with it and trying to read the directions that I think were written for PhD candidates in Information Technology.

I had gotten several messages from Alexis who sounded like she was in a state of panic about something. She wanted me to call her. I would take care of that later.

The ride to Milwaukee was pleasant enough. The kids have electronic games and screens and movies and all the rest of that stuff to keep them busy. When I was a kid I was allowed two comic books and then I had to look out the window. My mother was always under the impression that I would get carsick if I read while the car was moving.

We met Jennifer at Del Debbio's, a small family owned Italian restaurant with white tablecloths in downtown Milwaukee. It was perfect for an intimate Friday night date. I was thinking that I probably should have insisted on Chucky Cheese. Jennifer obviously didn't understand children. Maybe this was a mistake. I had no choice but to make the best of it.

Jennifer had arrived directly from the office. She was dressed as if she was going to close a major construction loan rather than heading to the zoo with two small children and their father who she had once slept with but hadn't seen in a year, as she insisted on pointing out a couple times. I think she was blaming her limited Milwaukee social life on me.

We engaged in semi-polite small talk. I was distracted by the kids who needed my attention as we ordered lunch. There wasn't much on the menu for them. Peanut butter and jelly would have been best. But, I got them to split a dish of spaghetti.

"Dad, you eat spaghetti for dinner, not lunch," Scotty told me.

"You're right. I just thought we would try something different."

"Are you my Daddy's new wife?" Nicole asked Jennifer.

"No." Jennifer looked at me for help.

"Jennifer and I are friends," I told Nicole.

Things seem to warm up the longer we were together. We drove out to the zoo in two cars. Jennifer wanted to be able to escape when she was ready. She could see this date was nothing more than helping me to take care of the kids. I was thinking of it more as reconnecting. I promised her that I would stay in better touch now that I was retired from baseball.

"How long are you going to stay retired? You couldn't have made that much money. You weren't that good." Thanks, I thought.

"Besides, you don't even have a resume. What can you do other than be a baseball coach?"

It did seem that everyone was quick to point this out to me. I kept thinking that I wanted to just say that "I'm going to walk the earth."

Samson was the hit of the zoo walk. He's an impressive animal. Nicole was mesmerized by Samson. They seemed to hit it off well, staring at each other through the glass. I figured Nicole will become an animal biologist someday. Jennifer even enjoyed the gorilla. She mentioned that Samson seemed to have the same traits as most of the men she dated, which obviously included me. She couldn't let it go.

After about two hours we were all ready to leave. I said goodbye to Jennifer in the parking lot promising her I would keep in touch. "Right! I'll hang by the phone," she commented. We did kiss but I guess it was more of a peck than anything. Of course, we were aware that the kids were watching.

I figured we would skip the Hasenpfeffer at Karl Ratzsch's. That was for another time. At the moment I could see a McDonald's in my future. The kids were tired. I was tired. Jennifer had made it clear that she had better things to do. We headed back to Chicago stopping at the Golden Arches at the Kenosha exit near the Illinois – Wisconsin border.

Being an occasional visitor in my kids' life was not easy. I knew for the ease of everyone that Bill would probably be a better father than me. He would be there. I wouldn't. Frankly, I didn't know where I would be, but I knew I had to stay in these kids' lives somehow. That's just how it was going to be. I dropped the kids off. Loretta wasn't there but Bill was. We shook hands and he wished me well. I knew he was a pretty good guy as much as I hated to admit it. I did feel this guy would help work things out and keep emotions on that side of the table in check. I told him I would be in touch.

CHAPTER

6

I left early the next morning. I hit I-55 heading south about 7 a.m. It's about a six-hour ride to St. Louis, which was my ultimate next stop. However, I wanted to have lunch in Springfield, the state capital and home of the Abraham Lincoln Presidential Library and Museum. It was about a four-hour drive. Despite the impression that Alexis seemed to have of dumb jocks, I actually considered myself somewhat of a history buff. There's so much literature available on Lincoln that it's hard not to become interested at some level. Stopping at the library and museum is the sort of thing I never got to do when I was playing ball. Springfield was an occasional minor league city when I was playing at that level. Of course, the museum wasn't built back in those days. Regardless, even if it had been I wouldn't have had the time to visit.

Minor league baseball consumes even more time than the major leagues. primarily because you travel on a bus. And, the coaches constantly work you on the fundamentals that you need to learn to get to the next level. Your life is pretty much eating, sleeping, playing baseball games and riding the bus.

About 9:30 a.m. I made a call to Alexis. It was an hour later in Cleveland, so I figured she was probably at work. I got her voice mail. Twenty miles later she called me back.

"I need to see you!"

"Okayyy…You know I'm in Illinois, right?"

"Yes. Walking the Earth."

"Right now, I happened to be driving the Earth." I was beginning to regret my little joke. Everyone seemed to throw this back at me.

"Joe is having an affair." I could tell she was distressed.

"So what? We've been having an affair for a long time. What's fair for the gander is fair for the goose."

"That's a fucking cliché, Rowe. Can't you get original?" She always had to edit my comments.

"How do you know he's having an affair?"

"He told me. He basically said the same thing you just said. He knew that you and I had been seeing each other. He didn't really seem to give a shit. So, he decided there was no reason he shouldn't do the same thing. Are you talking while driving? You should pull over. It's the safe thing to do."

"Yes, I'm talking while driving. Since when do you care about my safety?"

"I might be getting a divorce. You're next in line."

"Thanks. That's really endearing."

"What's your next stop?"

"St. Louis."

"Okay. I'll get a flight and meet you there."

"Well actually, it's not quite St. Louis. I'm going to see a friend of mine who coaches at a junior college in Illinois."

"Is that near St. Louis?"

"Alexis, you are the college graduate. I'm not. You're always reminding me of that. Are you serious that you don't know that Illinois is across the river from St. Louis?"

"Don't go big time on me. I'm in a very vulnerable state of mind at the moment. Okay. So when will you be in St. Louis?"

"Let me check out things with Ted and then I'll call you back."

"Okay. Goodbye." That was Alexis. Nothing sweet or endearing about it. When she was through talking she was through. I've never had any trouble developing relationships with women, but it was things like this that made me sure I would never get married again. At the same time, I was thinking that a couple days in a hotel in St. Louis might cure what ails both of us. I would be calling her back after I got to Ted Dover's house and figured out my plans.

I had also gotten a message from Tina to call her. I would call her later today after I did my Lincoln thing.

Springfield is what the big city journalists like to call a "sleepy town." It seems that every time some young scribe is sent out into the boondocks that the town is "sleepy." Alexis would probably even agree with my criticism. Despite her erratic temperament she was a dedicated professional journalist who religiously read Columbia Journalism Review and never lacked for a comment about what she perceived to be good and or bad journalism.

I always like to check out the local ballpark in any city I visit. Since I had played a few times in Springfield I particularly wanted to see Robin Roberts Stadium, named after Hall of Fame pitcher Robin Roberts, a Springfield native. Plus, it's located on the north side of town near Oak Ridge Cemetery and the Lincoln Tomb. This would be a twofer.

I recall that when I played there the stadium was desperately in need of rehab. There's been such a building boom in small town stadiums in recent years I was wondering how the place looked now. The stadium was now home to the Springfield Sliders, a summer college wooden bat league team.

I wasn't disappointed. The place didn't look too much different than when I played there. It was a good park for young prospects to hone their skills. If they made it up the ladder to the majors they would appreciate the quality of the fields, the clubhouse and the stadium amenities.

Oak Ridge Cemetery is just a few blocks away. I was amazed that I could just drive in, park and walk up to the tomb. There were no guards, just a couple other people walking around the tomb. Nobody had spray painted the tomb. No signs of vandalism. That would not be true in someplace like New York City where Grant's Tomb for years was a target of vandals. It's good to see that old Midwestern values still exist in places like Springfield.

I headed downtown, taking local streets through the neighborhoods. Neat frame houses, most of them painted white. The lawns were well tended. I found the museum about four blocks from the state capitol building. Springfield looked to me just like a Midwestern capital city should look. There are numerous state government buildings mixed in with a few upscale restaurants in town to serve the legislators. There's also the local "family restaurant" called The Chicago Grill where the local police and members of the chamber of commerce congregate for coffee and open-faced turkey sandwiches smothered in brown gravy.

I was hungry. It was time for lunch. So, The Chicago Grill was it. I took a booth along the side wall just underneath the picture window that gave me a view of the parking lot and the solid brick wall of the building next door.

I ordered a hamburger and fries with a vanilla milk shake, the All-American meal. Why not? If Alexis were here she would get all over me about healthy eating. She was uptight about almost everything in life, particularly food. So, when she wasn't around, I ate what I wanted to eat without guilt.

Even though I was not what you would call a star, people do tend to recognize me. My picture has been in newspapers, magazines and on television enough that a certain amount of the sporting public is bound to eventually figure out who I am in civilian clothes. My waitress Lilly, according to her name tag, turned out to be a big baseball fan.

"You're Stub Rowe, aren't you?" she asked when she returned with my food.

"Guilty as charged."

"What are you doing here? I thought you were in Cleveland."

"Ah. You must be one of my many fans," I commented in jest. "Just traveling through. The season is over, and I'm headed to St. Louis to see some friends."

"I remember when you played here. You went out with a friend of mine once."

"Who was that?" I had to be careful here. When you've played baseball in a lot of minor league towns there's always that chance that you left something or someone behind that you don't know about.

"Beebee Grossenbacher. She still talks about you and follows you in the newspaper all the time. Are you married?"

"Uh. No. Not anymore."

"She isn't either. You should give her a call."

"Why don't you just tell her I send my regards? I really have to keep moving."

"She works just down the street at the CVS Pharmacy. You could just stop by and say hello."

"I probably should keep going. I need to be in St. Louis later this afternoon." That wasn't true but so what.

I was hoping Lilly would go wait on some of her other customers. She didn't seem to be in much of a hurry though. Maybe no one in Springfield was in a hurry.

I was drawing a blank on BeeBee Grossenbacher. You would think that with a name like that I wouldn't forget her, but obviously I hadn't been too enthralled with our relationship. It would just add insult to injury if I had to meet face-to-face with BeeBee and didn't recognize her.

"Why are you in town?" I guess she didn't hear me when I said I was headed to St. Louis.

"Just passing through."

"I could show you around town if you want. Have you been to the Lincoln Museum? It's great. I get off after the lunch shift. That's all I work. I'll be done by 2."

I was beginning to see that this wasn't going to end. I did want to see the museum and it's always more fun seeing it with someone else. Lilly wasn't unattractive so, what the heck. Maybe I could hang around.

"Okay. It's a date," I said. "I have a couple errands to run and then I'll meet you at the museum at about 2:15. Does that work for you?"

"Sure. That's great. Are you going to stop by and see BeeBee?"

"Why don't we discuss that later?"

Lilly finally seemed to realize that she had other diners waiting for her service and went off to take care of them. I finished up, left a good tip, and told her I would see her in about an hour. I wasn't sure or not if I was going to show up. I could change my mind. But I thought I would take a little time and stroll around town. I did have some drug store items to buy but I thought it best to avoid CVS and the aforementioned BeeBee. I went out the door looking for a Walgreens.

At 2:15 p.m. sharp there was Lilly waiting for me. She had changed out of her waitress uniform. She was wearing a short and tight black skirt, flats and sleeveless polo shirt. She had redone her hair and makeup. Overall it was a pretty quick and efficient makeover. I would guess Lilly was about 30 to 35, and looked like she worked out. She had short dark hair. She had obviously spent time in the sun as her arms and face sported a healthy tan. On a baseball player's scale, she would rank a B plus.

"Hi. Did you go see BeeBee?"

"No. Why don't we just let the BeeBee thing ride? Sometimes it's best not to stir up old memories."

"Ah hah. Not so sure what you might have left behind. Right? Ah, baseball players..." She left the rest of her thought unsaid.

I treated her to the $12 admission charge which seemed a bit steep to me. But I guess it still qualifies as a cheap date. I couldn't really remember the last time I was in a museum where I had time to look around and read all the little tags underneath the exhibits. As I tried to read the small print with my nose against the glass I thought to myself that I probably had made the right decision about hanging up the glove and spikes. I wasn't seeing as well anymore.

We looked at old letters, photographs, books, belongings, clothing, furnishings, campaign posters, special exhibits, and just wandered. Lilly turned out to be a pretty good guide, well informed about the life of Lincoln, his friends, enemies and family, some of whom qualified as both friends and enemies. She told me she had been to the museum at least 20 times with her own family.

"Every time anyone from out of town visits they want to go to the museum. There aren't a lot of other things to do in Springfield," she explained. "So I figured I better learn to enjoy all this."

We stayed right up until the 5 p.m. closing time. That included browsing through the museum store where I bought a book called "Famous African-Americans in History." I bought Lilly a pink museum t-shirt. It seemed appropriate.

As we left the building I could feel her thinking, "Now what?"

"Seems to me it's cocktail time. Can I buy you a drink?"

"Sure. Rafferty's is just down the street. Let's go there."

She didn't bother to ask me about my need to get to St. Louis. She knew that was B.S. from the start; things were moving along between her and me so why ruin a good thing.

Rafferty's was decorated as an Irish pub, lots of dark wood, big booths and a long bar that dominated one side of the room. We plopped down in a booth and each ordered a Guinness. I always order Guinness and watch to see if the bartender knows what he's doing. The right way to pour a Guinness from the tap is to pour the beer down the sides until the glass is a bit over half full, then you wait an exact 1 minute and 18 seconds…yes, an exact one minute and 18 seconds to allow the foam to settle, and then top off the glass.

If you order a Guinness and it is delivered to you in anything fewer than three minutes, then you know they didn't do it right. I always find that the right time for a Guinness to show up is just about when you begin wondering if it will show up. They did it right at Rafferty's.

We clinked glasses. I thanked her for the tour. I had enjoyed it and found Lilly to be a welcome companion. She seemed to know when to talk and when to keep her mouth shut. I guess this came from giving multiple tours.

People usually want to ask me lots of questions about baseball and who I know and don't know. I sort of get tired of that routine, so I have learned to ask questions about them and their lives instead. Most people are impressed that I would even care, which believe it or not, I do. Baseball is just a job that gets reported on in the newspaper or on TV each day. We are people with short career spans. We have all the same issues as anyone else. We have financial challenges, family issues, mental health disorders. You name it. We got it.

Lilly's last name was Rogers. She had grown up in Springfield. She told me she had been married once, no children. She and her ex-husband were high school sweethearts. He was in the military.

"I lived with him at Fort Hood, Texas and later at Fort Benning, that's in Georgia, when he was in Ranger training," she told me. "But it's a tough life being a soldier's wife. It just wasn't for me. I missed my family. Mark was gone half the time. When he was home he was exhausted. We both knew it wasn't an appropriate time to have a family. He was a corporal making about $2,000 a month. We were always scrambling for money. Our folks had to help us out on occasion. I usually had a waitress job. There are plenty of those in a military town, but it was never enough.

"But Mark really enjoyed the army. That's where he wanted to be. Eventually, we just decided that the marriage wasn't going to work. So I came home. No hard feelings. We stay in touch. Right now, he's on his third tour in Afghanistan.

"I think he has a new girlfriend, but nothing serious. I wish him well."

Lilly didn't seem to be the type to get too wound up about anything, so I could see her making that sort of decision without casting any blame. That would never happen with someone like Alexis who seemed to blame weather changes on her husband.

We continued to chat and eventually decided to have something to eat. Lilly was easy to be with, I enjoyed the company and began to think that staying over was a possibility.

When we finished dinner, we decided to take a walk. She said there was an ice cream shop down the street. The weather outside was still pleasantly early fall. We had light jackets that we carried rather than wearing them. I took her hand when we crossed the street and we continued holding hands into the ice cream store.

I've always been a vanilla man myself, which opens me to lots of snickering from friends and loved ones who think that's a boring choice. Lilly ordered peach fondue, two scoops. Eating an ice cream cone and having a conversation at the same time takes a certain amount of concentration to do it right or else you have a mess on your hands. Lilly was very good at it. A lick here and there, turning the cone at just the right time to catch the side that was melting the fastest. In between she was able to get in a few comments, questions or a giggle that I decided was definitely girl cute.

I sort of attack ice cream cones. I bite into them even though it causes my teeth to hurt. Hey, I'm a professional baseball player, or used to be. I can handle pain. It's a small price to pay for the flavor of good vanilla.

We talked about news events, the war, some politics, life in Springfield, a trip she took with her sister to New York last year. We shared a cup of coffee after the ice cream. Neither one of us wanted the evening to end.

Finally, she asked the question I hadn't really been thinking about. "Where are you staying tonight? Surely you aren't going to St. Louis now, are you?"

"I guess the time has slipped away. I've enjoyed being with you. Thanks. I don't know, I guess I'll just get a hotel room and head out tomorrow morning."

"You can stay with me if you want."

I didn't say anything. I know I had a puzzled smile on my face.

"Really," she said. "I would like you to."

"I don't want to put you out." That seemed like the polite thing to say, and the proper thing to say. You can't jump too quickly at an offer like this.

"C'mon. Let's go home." She took my hand and out we went to my car. I dropped her off at the restaurant where she had left her car. Then I followed her to her house, which took about 15 minutes. She owned a townhouse in a newer development on the west side of town.

Living room, small dining area and kitchen on the first floor with a powder room. Three bedrooms on the second floor with a full bath. The tiniest bedroom, and I mean tiny, was more of an office and junk area.

There was a guest bedroom, but I was figuring by this time that I wasn't going to be sleeping there. She poured us each a glass of Bailey's and we sat on the couch watching the evening newscast.

"Thanks again for showing me around today. This was as nice a day I've had since the end of the season," I told her.

I realized it had just been 10 days since I had made my final out that would be entered into the Baseball Encyclopedia. My new life was just getting started. There would be no off-season workouts. I didn't have to lift weights, run miles, take batting practice, keep the arm limber, stay away from motorcycles or skydiving, not that I wanted to do those things anyways. But you never know.

She leaned over and kissed me. I didn't resist. I never resist. There's no resisting in baseball. I kissed her back and we began to breathe heavier. I guess you could say that we necked for a few minutes. That term, necked, seems like something out of high school in the '60s, but, that's what we did. Foreplay sounds better. She took my hand and led me upstairs to the master bedroom which featured a queen-sized bed.

She had it decorated with what seemed like about 20 throw pillows. This was not the first bedroom I've been in that we had to dispose of the throw pillows before proceeding to business. I've never quite understood why women feel those are necessary. They just end up in a pile on the floor.

There were a few photos on the bureau. There was one of Lilly in her wedding dress with Mark in his uniform. I guess Mark was going to be watching us.

"I'll be just a couple minutes," Lilly said as she went in the bathroom. "Make yourself at home." There was a very mischievous smile that accompanied that remark.

Okay. I guess that was an invitation to take my clothes off and jump in her bed. I've done that before. I don't have to be told twice. Being a professional baseball player has its perks.

I turned the bed down, then the lights followed. I crawled in and waited. She came back in about five minutes wearing absolutely nothing. I liked this girl. She just got down to business.

She walked over to the bureau and took her earrings off. There was no shyness here about being naked with a guy she had known for less than a half a day. She had a great body. Maybe some people might think she was a bit on the skinny side, but I would just call her fit. There was no excess. Her breasts were small but round and firm. Her nipples were erect. All in all, I was impressed.

There was a light next to the bed that I had turned down to gives us some atmosphere. She turned it back up to maximum. Must have been at least a hundred watts.

"Let's leave the lights on so we can see each other," she said climbing under the covers.

"Sure," I answered. It was her house, her bed. We would do what she wanted. We snuggled, and it wasn't long before her hand began to softly fondle me. Then she started to kiss me, first around the ear, then on my neck and then the chest. All the while she was continuing with the great hand action. She was in charge here. That was okay by me.

"Do you mind if I give you a blow job?" she asked.

Now that stopped me in my tracks. No one had ever asked me that before. Is there any other answer than "hell yes?" In my past sexual relationships getting a blow job was like winning the lottery. It just didn't happen that often. I was beginning to wonder if I had entered the Twilight Zone and this wasn't really me. I was thinking that a commercial would come on soon and I would wake up to an unfulfilled erection.

But no. This was real. This was beginning to be every man's greatest dream. This was not a woman who sat back and waited for me to do everything. She was totally engaged in the process.

I was trying not to have an orgasm as I didn't want to waste it at that moment. Lilly sensed that I was getting close so she came up for air. "Maybe we'll leave the rest for later," she said with a smile. This girl knew what she was doing.

She reached over to the night stand, pulled open the drawer and pulled out a condom.

"We probably should use this." She was better than me at tearing open the little package which I usually had to rip open with my teeth. I don't know if other guys feel this way or not, but I have always felt that there was something particularly erotic about a woman putting a condom on me.

She slowed me down, then when she thought the time was right she got on top and started making love to me. So, this is what it's like to be on the bottom. Almost immediately she started making sounds that I had never experienced before other than in a porno movie. Lilly wasn't doing this for a film crew. This was really her totally involved and in command. She included grunts, dirty words, heavy breathing, little screeches, sighs, whines and screams. Go for it girl. She was having what appeared to me to be one orgasm after another.

She made me feel like the world's greatest stud. Before long I was matching her sounds. This was the first time I had ever just let go like this. I made up new words and noises as we went along.

When I was riding the buses in the minor leagues with a lot of other horny young guys, we read and passed around what we called "fuck books," short, paperback novels that we bought at adult book stores. They were thinly thought out plots that were just an excuse to feature sex scenes once every 10 pages. To kill time on the interminable bus rides we would often read passages out loud to each other. Terms like "heaving loins" and "orgasmic eruptions" described the sex acts. None of us really believed these things could occur in real life.

With other women, including my ex-wife, an orgasm was something they seemed to experience about once a year, like at Christmas. Most other times they would tell me: "I enjoyed the hugging."

Finally, I couldn't hold back any longer. I'm not sure how long we had been at this, five, ten minutes. It could have been an hour. Then I had what I was the longest orgasm in my life. I got a slight cramp in my thigh and it felt like blood was sucked from my toes. I was living a fuck book. Lilly had turned up the volume of her noises. Through all this I became aware that the bedroom windows were open, and I was sure someone would call the police thinking that a homicide was taking place.

As the tempo slowed we lowered our volume to deep sighs and moaning. One of us said "Oh my God." I'm not sure who that was but I was hoping it was Lilly. I was exhausted. I had a tough time imagining the follow-up blow job she had hinted at earlier.

We were on our backs and didn't say anything to each other. After a couple minutes I sensed that she was beginning to move and make little sounds.

"I hope you don't mind but I like to pleasure myself," she said.

Holy Moly. I thought I had just given my greatest effort of all times and it wasn't enough. This was never in the fuck books or porno movies. The girl was always more than satisfied. I would have preferred that she had said: "I enjoyed the hugging."

She knew what I was thinking and reached over with her spare hand to touch me. "Don't worry. It was great. I just need a little more." With mixed emotions I watched Lilly come to another climax which I sensed that she enjoyed more than she did with me.

"Whew," she said and smiled at me. She leaned over and kissed me. "That was fun. Thanks." I can't remember ever being thanked before.

We talked a bit. We touched. She fondled me, not herself. Time passed and eventually she fulfilled her earlier promise to me. Then we fell asleep.

CHAPTER 7

I woke up with the sun pounding through the window which obviously faced east. Lilly was up and gone. I never heard her. She worked the breakfast and lunch shifts at the diner. She left a message on the counter.

"The coffee is on. Help yourself to whatever you can find in the fridge. Or come on down to The Chicago Grill for breakfast. Hope to see you again. LOL Lil."

Nice and simple. I decided that Lilly was an uncomplicated woman who was probably low maintenance in both the short and long run. I didn't sense any hidden agendas.

I scratched myself for a minute in the place that men always scratch in the morning. I poured a cup of coffee and sat at the counter thinking about last night, about where I should go today and what my situation was with Lilly.

I hadn't paid any attention in the last couple of days to my phone, so it seemed like a good time to see if I had any messages.

Since Alexis usually sent me four or five a day I knew I would have several from her. Sometimes I hated to turn the damn thing on because it would probably just be another crisis.

The first message was from my sister that just said: "Call me when you can. Need to talk." Alexis, of course, had called, e-mailed and texted. Everything but smoke signals. Her tone ranged from "I miss you and think of you always" to "where are you? – you son of a bitch" and "who are you fucking now?" I've never seen a time pattern to Alexis' state of mind. She can get out of bed sweet as pie or angry as an alley cat. Part of the value of this trip was to just get away from Alexis.

There was an e-mail from my agent, Hub Collins, suggesting a few speaking gigs and wondered if I was available. That was an easy "no." I said "thanks for thinking of me but I'm presently walking the earth. I'll call you, don't call me."

I would have liked to have called the kids, but I knew they were in school. I didn't want to call Alexis because I would just get interrogated.

I flipped through about 50 e-mails hitting the delete button. There were the NY Times news bulletins, now mostly old news even though I hadn't exactly been keeping up, but most of the news I had already heard from one source or another. I got a couple messages from the ex-prince of Nigeria who needed me to send him my bank account number, so I could help him get his throne back and in return he promised me millions. Nah, I don't think so. There were a couple pornographic solicitations that had gotten through the spam filter, some travel deals from cruise lines, and a few jokes from an old high school buddy that was sent to at least 40 people on his address list. This technology has become such an essential part of our life but when I really measure the value of what I would miss without it, well, not too much.

I called Tina hoping she would tell me to come to Indianapolis and kill her husband.

"Hi Hon. It's Kenny. How are you?"

"Kenny! Kenny!" That's all she could say. I could tell she had been crying.

"What's going on?"

"I don't know what's going on. That's the problem."

"Want me to come over there and kill Bob?" She didn't' answer immediately. That's a good sign.

"He's been gone the past two nights. He comes home during the day, sleeps for a while, doesn't really say where he's been or what he's been doing. Then he leaves again. He gave me over $6,000 in cash. In cash! Told me to go pay the bills. All he said is that he has some deals going. I don't know what the hell to think."

"Well, maybe he does have some deals going." I decided not to say that "maybe he robbed a bank as well." I thought it was funny, but I knew Tina wouldn't. She was upset enough without my offbeat humor about her deadbeat husband.

"I don't know. I don't know what to think. I'm just confused and he's not telling me what's going on. I just have a bad feeling."

I really didn't want to drive to Indianapolis for a false alarm. I was sure it was just more of Bob's goofiness at work. And, as much as I loved Tina and would always be there for her, she had to work this out herself. If things got really bad then I would go and see what I could do.

"Tina, I'm driving down to St. Louis this afternoon. I'll be in touch. If you need me I can be in Indianapolis in 4 or 5 hours. Not a big deal. But, see if you can't work this out. How are the kids?"

"They're okay. Bob never pays much attention to them, but there's nothing new about that."

"Okay, honey. I'll be in touch. You can call me anytime. I have to hit the road right now."

After we hung up the phone I took a shower, made the bed and repacked my suitcase. When I told Tina I was leaving for St. Louis that had made up my mind to stick to my agenda and not get too waylaid.

I liked Lilly and felt I wanted to see her again. It wasn't just the sex although that was spectacular. She just seemed to appeal to my need for an uncomplicated relationship. I decided to head down to the diner for a late breakfast, or an early lunch, whatever it was.

When I came in the door I saw her near the back of the dining room waiting on a couple of grubby looking guys. One had on a red hat with a logo for DeKalb Seeds. The other was wearing the green and yellow colors of John Deere. She was pouring them coffee while they were looking intently on their menus. I wondered if they could read or if they may have gotten a special menu with pictures, so they could just point.

I know, that's terrible of me to make assumptions about two guys who probably worked harder in a week than I had in two years.

There was an open booth near the front and I slipped into it. I had bought a USA Today newspaper out front as I hate sitting in a restaurant by myself without something to read.

Lilly came over. "Hi, honey."

Whoa, let's not jump to conclusions here, I thought, although I think she meant it in a more generic way. Waitresses call everyone honey.

"Did you sleep okay? Coffee?" She poured. "I wasn't sure if I would see you again."

"Slept great. Thanks for putting up with me. I would like to see you again, but I do have to head to St. Louis today."

"Sure. I understand. You were headed there yesterday. You need to keep on your schedule. Are you going to have something to eat?"

"Why not? Two eggs, over easy, hash browns and rye toast."

"Yes sir. Coming right up." She smiled and threw me a wink. I sort of melted. There is something serendipitous about the day after great sex with a new lover.

She was too busy to spend any extra time with me. She was a professional waitress and she wasn't going to let personal issues cloud her performance. I watched as she juggled orders from 8 different tables and booths, smoothly working in coffee refills. She chatted briefly with each table but kept moving.

People talk about what a difficult job it is being a waitress…or waiter. She was constantly on the move. Like most people that come to a restaurant I had taken for granted the service that I felt was due me. But I gained respect for the profession as I watched her multi-task and treat everyone as if they were her best friend. I figured that even in Springfield she was at the top of the tip chart. If she was working at Morton's Steak House in Chicago she'd make 100 grand a year.

She brought my order over, refilled the coffee and asked if there was anything else I needed. Her coy smile told me that she was thinking the same thing I was, that what she had provided last night would go well this morning with breakfast. Ah…dreamers.

"You're working hard. No help today?"

"Funny you should mention that. Nancy, the other girl, called in sick today, or I think

maybe one of her kids was sick. Doesn't matter. I can handle it."

I finished off the eggs and the USA Today in about the same amount of time. Lilly circled back with more coffee. "Will you keep in touch?"

"Of course. Give me your e-mail."

"Fungirl1984@yahoo.com."

I saved it into my address book and immediately sent her an e-mail, so she would be able to capture my address. "Lilly – thanks again. I appreciated the tour, dinner and your letting me stay over. LOL Stub." I decided to avoid the references to our sexual activities and focus on things that made us sound like friends. I was sincere about staying in touch although I wasn't sure if she believed me or not. I could see myself making a return road trip just to see Lilly.

She waved at me as I left the restaurant. "Bye bye. Love ya," I said in return. The "love ya" is just a friendly expression. It was meant that way and I'm sure she took it that way. But it was a way of saying that our relationship could be more than just a one-night stand.

I headed on down I-55. It would be about two hours to St. Louis. Ted Dover lived in Belleville, on the Illinois side of the river. Belleville is best known for being the hometown of former professional tennis champion Jimmy Connors.

Ted is the baseball coach at the local community college and teaches PE classes as well. To supplement his income, he teaches drivers education at the local high school. I called him once I was on the road to let him know I would be showing up later today and to make sure it was okay with him and Mrs. Dover, who I had never met.

Ted and I played together in the low minor leagues. We both signed originally with the White Sox organization. He was an outfielder without much bat, arm or speed. His time in professional ball was bound to be short. He knew that also but felt it would be good experience to pass on to his players in future years. Ted had always wanted to be a coach more than he wanted to be a player. His contract got sold once to the Pirates. They kept him for one season and then declined to invite him back the next year. His career lasted less than two years.

But he had been good about keeping in touch. Besides the obligatory Christmas cards, he would attend a few games a year. We would always have dinner or lunch, whatever fit the schedule.

Once we were playing in Kansas City when his JUCO team was in a regional playoff. He had me come over and talk to the team, sort of a Knute Rockne pump 'em up speech. They lost the game 9 to 2. I guess I didn't do a very good job.

I took my time getting to Belleville. I didn't want to arrive until dinner time. Ted was working, and I thought it would be awkward for me and the missus to be sitting around chatting without Ted being there. It's amazing all the things you can find to do when you need to waste some time. I remember seeing a movie with John Travolta called "Michael" where he wanted to see the world's largest ball of twine. I felt that I was on a similar mission.

I drove over to Wood River to see the monument marking the spot that Lewis & Clark left from on their famous expedition up the Missouri River in 1803. No one knows how much I have read about history. People like Alexis and Jennifer just assume I'm a dumb jock. But, when you travel as much as I did in baseball there was plenty of downtime and I couldn't watch TV all the time, so I did a lot of reading.

Little known fact about Stub Rowe, I visited libraries and art museums in every city that I played. No one ever recognized me. Who would expect to see a major league ballplayer in their local library?

I drove the River Road up to Alton and looked around. It's an interesting old river town which is located at the confluence of the Mississippi, Missouri and Illinois Rivers. According to the official history of Alton, it was home to Native Americans for several centuries which is evidenced by archaeological artifacts and a prehistoric bird painted on a cliff face nearby and written about in 1673 by French missionary priest Father Jacques Marquette.

Look it up. It's all on Wikipedia.

Ted had e-mailed me directions to his house. I also have GPS although I have to admit that I'm a bit of a snob about that device. I have always used maps quite efficiently and feel that I can find anything without some electronic gizmo directing me. Plus, I have found a few times when the GPS lady was wrong, confused and completely disoriented. Once, during spring training in Florida I was looking for a Sonny's Barbecue Restaurant. I love their pulled pork sandwiches with the hot barbecue sauce.

I plugged Sonny's into the GPS and let the lady take me there. About two blocks before the restaurant she instructed me to turn into what was obviously a toxic material dump site. It was fenced in featuring signs that warned of dangerous materials inside.

I arrived at Ted's shortly before 6 p.m. His home was in a modern subdivision of Belleville. It was a two-story frame and brick, with attached garage and a small, well-landscaped front yard. It looked just like millions of other modern homes built in the past 20 years in America's suburbs.

I can imagine the subdivision sales rep now: "Would you like the Georgian Colonial with the Presidential Bathroom package or the Tudor Country style with the Queen Anne Kitchen?"

Ted had heard my car come into the driveway, so he came out to meet me followed by a seemingly friendly black Labrador and a small blond haired boy. This was a photo op right out of an insurance company commercial. At any second I expected a over voice to say: "What would happen to your family if something unexpected happened to you? Will they be taken care of in an emergency? Call today for a free brochure."

"Hey Stub. Great to see you. C'mon in. C'mon in, buddy." It had been about three years since I had seen Ted. He hadn't changed much. As a coach and PE teacher he had the opportunity to stay in shape.

I was quickly introduced to his son Josh who I had guessed correctly was 6, his wife Amy, and the dog Lucky. Two other children, eight-year-old twin daughters Laura and Lindsay, were expected home from swimming practice shortly.

Amy was a cute, short, slightly plump blond who gave me a big hug even though we had never met before. Some people are just like that. They are huggers. I came from a family that was a little more restrained in that area. We always offered a handshake first, but I could go for the hugging if I saw the other person was that way.

We went into the den. Josh joined us. Ted offered me a soft drink. I was thinking more about a beer. He obviously saw the surprise on my face.

"Sorry, Stub. I probably should have told you. I don't drink anymore. Amy and I are born again. We gave up the evil brews a few years ago."

"Then a Coke will do," I said.

"Pepsi only."

"That's what I really wanted. A Pepsi."

"I'll join you. How about a slice of lime in it?"

"Sure. Why not. I'm not driving." Oh boy. This could be an interesting visit. Ted went into the kitchen to get the refreshments. Amy, Josh and I participated in small talk about my trip to Belleville, the tour of Wood River and Alton. I mentioned stopping in Springfield to see the Lincoln Museum but skipped the subject of Lilly.

"How long are you in town for, Stub?" Amy asked. "We have your room ready for you."

"I don't want to be any bother to you. Overnight. Thought Ted and I could get caught up. I wanted to meet you guys. See how you're doing."

"Ted says you're just taking a tour?

I wanted to tell her that I was walking the earth until God told me to stop. As a Christian she probably would buy into it. But, I decided to low key my plans.

"Just need to get away from baseball for a while and think about what I'm going to do next. I get lots of great ideas when I just have myself to talk to during these long drives."

"I'm sure God will be with you all the way and help you with your decision. Just let Him decide," Amy said.

"Okay. Good advice," I responded.

I looked around the house as we chatted. The place was filled with religious symbols, the famous framed photo of Jesus that seems to be in every Christian household was hung prominently over the mantle.

Amy announced that dinner was about ready and suggested to Josh that he should show me my room and perhaps I would want to freshen up before we ate.

The guest bedroom was similarly decorated in a manner that I could not forget God. I went into the closet to hang up a couple shirts and pair of pants out of my suitcase. The closet was in perfect order. Everything was on plastic hangers.

Whenever I see plastic hangers I think of my first "real" girlfriend, Melody Wise, who I hadn't seen now for about 14 years. It was the one year I spent at community college and she invited me home for a weekend to her parent's house. Just like today I went to hang up my clothes in the closet and it was the first time I had ever seen plastic hangers.

My mother was so frugal that she would never consider buying hangers when she got them for free at the dry cleaners. I figured Melody's parents must have been very wealthy to be able to afford hangers like that.

Loretta bought plastic hangers for our house. They only cost about a dime apiece. It was the first time I realized that middle class people could also afford plastic hangers. But, then again, who needs 'em? My mother was right.

I knew that as soon as we sat down we were going to have to say grace. I knew my old joke of "Yeah God. Thanks for the grub. Let's eat," wouldn't do it. I was the guest, so I needed to go along with their customs. I don't think I had said grace in about 10 years.

By the time I got down to the dining room the twins were home. They were adorable, bubbly and polite. They were also identical. After the introductions they moved around and there was no way I could keep track of who was who. I think Lindsay was wearing a blue shirt and Laura was wearing red, so I tried to keep track by associating the R in Laura with the R in red.

As predicted we all had to hold hands around the table, bow our heads and Ted said grace thanking the Lord for bringing an old friend to their family, asking for protection for our American soldiers overseas, and a blessing of the entire family and by the time he got through I think it included the entire St. Louis Metropolitan Statistical Area.

Amy was a devoted home economist who made nutritious meals for her family three times a day always asking the Lord to bless the food "of which we are about to consume," et cetera. Okay, enough of the Jesus stuff, that's all I could think.

The Dovers always had their children tell them about their day.

"Well, we got to school, took off our hats and coats, stood for the pledge..."

I was dying for a beer and thinking what a major mistake this was. I should have called Alexis and had her meet me for a wild sexual weekend in St. Louis. After the night with Lilly I was pumped and ready to go and here I was now spending a day and night in Sunday School. I could have just met Ted for a cup of coffee. I guess I forgot how real families spend their time. Then again, I wasn't sure if this was a real family or something created by God and Hollywood. They were like perfect. I got to doubting myself as a father and family man.

But I was here and there was no getting out of it. After the kids told about their days Amy, Ted and I participated in polite small talk about our lives. They asked about the baseball season just concluded and who I thought would win the World Series, who were the top players now, were steroids still a thing in the locker rooms. That was the closest we got to controversy.

They told me about their last family vacation and that now they were looking forward to going to Disney World next year. Ugh. Could this get any more boring? Holy shit. The night before this I had spent with Lilly in one of the greatest sexual events of my life, and now this.

I helped Amy with the dishes just to be the good guest while Ted started getting the kids ready for bed. He would be consumed for the next hour in reading to them as well.

Afterwards the three adults watched television. As Ted switched the stations he stopped for a few minutes to watch some evangelist. I was sure we would end up watching that the rest of the night. But, eventually he moved on to the ESPN. Thank God for 24-hour sports.

It was one of the most boring nights of my life. About 9:30 I excused myself saying I had had a long day and was tired. The Dovers were both early to bed, early to rise people so I knew it was appropriate. In my room there was a lot of religious literature on the book shelves.

Having been on the road all those years in baseball I had become an avid reader and always had three or four books with me. I had already started Jon Krakauer's "Into the Wild" which somehow, I had missed before. The trick to travel and books is to have something that's easy to get in to. You don't want to be reading "War and Peace."

I had recently bought my first Kindle and although I was initially against reading on a screen I had gotten used to it without too much trouble. In theory I was saving money by downloading books for $9.95 each rather than buying the hard copies for two or three times as much. But, what I found was that I was buying a lot more books than I could read. They were backed up in my queue. Regardless, my reading needs were taken care of without resorting to the Dovers' religious literature.

I slept well and woke a little before 6 a.m. I could smell coffee brewing and heard some muffled talking. I did a few ablutions in the bathroom, threw on my sweat pants and golf shirt, and headed down to join the family.

I found them all in serious group prayer. Ted, the titular head of household, was reading from the bible while the family all knelt on cushions, heads bowed, eyes closed, and hands folded together. I really wasn't sure of the protocol. I stood watching from the kitchen which opened into the family room where they were all kneeling. I was literally an arm's length from the coffee which was beckoning to me.

Ted became aware of my presence. He looked up and waved me into the room. "Our precious Lord, we thank you for bringing our friend Stub Rowe to us at this time. We ask him to join us as we pray together and look for your blessings and forgiveness."

Talk about an awkward moment. I probably hadn't been to church in 20 years and I sure hadn't been a part of any prayer group. Every team I was on had its share of bible thumpers who would hold prayer meetings when we were on road trips. Like evangelists anywhere they were always trying to recruit. Most of us preferred sticking to our present lifestyle which included alcohol, easy women and recreational drugs, at least before they started testing for those things – the drugs, that is.

Oh well, there's a first time for anything. One of the twins, how would I know which one, pulled a cushion off the couch and placed it next to her. Then she held out her hand to me. It was cute. It was hard to decline. Okay. I knelt. I held her hand. Amy was on the other side and she took my other hand in hers. Now we were all connected through this chain of hands. Ted moved on to some reading that had something to do with goats, mountains, wine and salvation.

Every now and then the whole group would sort of mumble together "amen." I wasn't sure how they got their cues, but they were in sync with each other. I would follow up late with a word that sounded more like "ahm."

Then Ted fell silent. The whole group fell silent. Our palms were sweaty. Or at least mine was. I was afraid to look around, but I peeked. They all had their heads bowed.

After about 25 seconds of what I assumed to be silent prayer, they all stood and picked up the cushions. Amy hugged me. "Thank you so much for joining us this morning. It means so much to us." She had tears in her eyes as she kissed my cheek.

"Uh. Okay. Sure. I'm glad I could join you." It didn't exactly come out smoothly. I stumbled over the words. Did I say the right thing? This was now even more awkward than I would have imagined it to be.

Every meal at the Dovers' house was a family affair. Breakfast was no different. Even though we had just finished a group prayer we all said grace as we sat down to our cereal, muffins and juice. It was a simple but healthy breakfast.

"Stub, are you going with Ted this morning? I'm sure he would love to have you there," Amy said.

I looked at Ted. Nothing had been said but I assumed my visit included a tour of the community college athletic facilities. Ted acknowledged that he expected me to go with him.

"Sure. Looking forward to it," I said. "What time did you want to leave? I should check my e-mails."

Ted said one hour. He also had a few things to take care too.

After breakfast I went to my room. I had been ignoring the e-mails and the phone messages I had been getting. I meant for this trip to have some element of that, but I knew I couldn't just ignore them forever.

I fired up my smart phone and first checked the CNN news feed. The lead story, ironic as it may seem since I was in an ultra-Christian household, that famous evangelist Rev. Lenny Kyser, had tearfully admitted an addiction to pornography. His mega-church is in southeastern Michigan, near Detroit, where his appeal to out-of-work automobile industry workers was due to a ministry based on the idea that Jesus had been a member of the union.

He was outed by a community newspaper reporter who moonlighted at a local video store. It turns out that the Rev. Kyser was renting his own movies although usually he appeared in disguise. The good reverend seemed to favor porno movies featuring large, well actually fat, actresses. The term for this fetish was "chubby chasers."

A video of his television confession was attached to the story. In less than 24 hours it had become the most watched video on You Tube. The good reverend, with his dutiful and somewhat overweight wife, was standing in the background holding her bible and moving her lips in prayer.

"I have sinned," he blubbered. "I ask God for his forgiveness. I am a human being given to flaws. Pray for me."

Interviews with a few of his parishioners indicated they didn't think this was that big a deal. I certainly got the impression that the adult movie video store could still be a viable business in that area of the country. I guess they didn't know they could just download this stuff to their laptop computers.

Alexis had sent me several more e-mails, text and phone messages. The only thing she hadn't tried so far was smoke signals. I decided I would call her. Despite her high maintenance, I sort of missed her. And ever since I had left Lilly – what was that? just two days ago now – I kept thinking about sex with Alexis. Our time in bed together had always been an athletic adventure. After Lilly I wanted to see how Alexis would stack up.

She answered her phone on the second ring. "Well, well, well. What do I owe the pleasure of a phone call from the formerly lame jock, Stub Rowe?"

I ignored her sarcasm. "Hi, sweetie. How have you been?"

There was a long pause on her end. Long for Alexis is 5 or 6 seconds. I wasn't sure what to expect. You never know with someone who is bipolar. If she had been taking her medication all would be fine. In fact, she would be mellow. If not, this call wouldn't last long.

"Where the fuck are you?" That was said her mellow tone.

"Near St. Louis. Did you want to come down for a few days?"

"St. Louis? Now why would I want to come to St. Louis? What possibly could be in St. Louis that I would want to leave my husband and come there to spend my vacation time with my fuck jockey."

"No problem. I understand. They do have some pretty good restaurants here. We could just hang out." The strategy with Alexis was to ignore her confrontational attitude. She couldn't help the fact that she was an asshole. The only reason I continued our relationship was that she was exciting, a great sex partner, and when in her infrequent good moods was actually charming, funny and her intellect is far superior to mine. That was attractive to me.

"I'll get a flight out this afternoon. Joe is in Baltimore for the weekend. He's covering the Browns game with the Ravens." I had gotten used to Alexis' instantaneous changes in moods and decision making. I would have been surprised if she had said that she couldn't come. I had learned over the two years of our relationship that usually she would do what I wanted her to do, I just had to take some shit before she would agree.

Alexis had three or four phones. She was talking to me on one of them while going on line with her smart phone to book a ticket. "I can be there at 4:47 p.m. American Airlines Flight 337. Meet me at baggage claim. Luv ya!" She hung up.

Ted and I left for his office about 9:30 a.m. "This is my off-season," he told me. "We start getting serious just before Christmas and then we have 6 a.m. practices in the gym. It's about the only time we can get in there. We have a batting cage in the basement and I'm working with kids at 5 a.m. almost every day."

The Mustangs, as they are called, played 76 games between February and June when the JUCO season ended. Ted then coaches a college wooden bat league team which plays another 60 games during the summer. He's away from home during the season about half the nights, or more than 100 for road games.

On the side, he gives private lessons throughout the year to players as young as 12. He tutors a few legitimate pro prospects and even has a couple major leaguers that come to him at times for specific help. He's developed a reputation in the industry as being one of the top amateur coaches and instructors. It's not easy but he seems to love it and doesn't complain about the pay which is modest. He told me he makes about $70,000 a year. Some top major leaguers make almost that much for a game.

I decided that I didn't love baseball that much to spend my entire life learning the best way to hit a ball with a piece of wood. I admire Ted for what he does but it's not for me.

He showed me around the facilities. I gave them a B. Compared to what we are used to in the major leagues, there is no comparison, but from what I experienced in high school and my one year of junior college ball, this was a definite upgrade.

The school fitness center was just beginning to make its appearance on the campus when I signed my first pro contract. We also didn't have many female athletes in those days, and as Ted and I toured the weight and exercise rooms I couldn't help but notice the number of women who were doing some serious weight lifting.

"Things have changed, Stub. Title IX made some significant changes. A lot of coaches and administrators fought it big time, but what it has done is not only leveled the playing field for all the teams and schools, but it has created jobs for coaches that never existed before.

"Women's crew teams have been the big thing in recent years. It doesn't cost a lot for a few boats. The girls don't have to be great athletes. But, it's given us the opportunity to meet our female quotas. Coaches were hard to find at first, but after a while the supply began to meet the demand."

"Aren't there problems with the male coach and female athlete?" I asked. He knew what I meant.

"Sure. We've had those problems. Always will. Love and sex. Or is it sex and love? Or maybe just sex. Whatever. The A.D. must keep a constant eye on that. Plus, there's the lesbian factor."

"Do you have any plans about moving up to an A.D. spot?"

"I'm pretty happy doing what I'm doing. Of course, I could use the money, but Amy and I make do. If we made more, we probably would just give it to the church."

This guy was too good to be true. I almost thought I could see a glow surrounding him. I'll bet he and his kids all have perfect teeth, too.

He introduced me around to the other coaches, administrators and even a janitor or two. There was no question Ted was well liked and respected. He had built a solid athletic program and being the Christian that he was, there was no cheating, no scandal, and everyone who dealt with him and his players knew that everything was on the up and up.

Ted is such an admirable guy it made me sick. It was time to get out of here and get back to being marginally moralistic or in whatever category I would fit. I thanked him for putting me up for the night and said all the cordial things you are supposed to say about a guy who had a great family, gave himself freely to the church and community and was successful in his chosen profession. Gag. We promised to keep in touch.

I could hardly wait to hit the road. Of course, I wasn't going far. Just to the St. Louis airport to meet Alexis and have a weekend of sex, drinking, fighting and more sex. I felt God understood my needs as well as Ted Dover's.

CHAPTER

8

I had a few hours to kill in St. Louis area waiting for Alexis. I went up in the Arch and checked out the view of the Mighty Mississippi, Illinois and Missouri. There is a very vulnerable feeling to being up in that thing. You are sort of jammed in with these tiny windows to look through. But, when in St. Louis…do as the tourists do.

I dawdled over lunch reading what seemed like every word in the Wall Street Journal. The way they cover the business news gives you this feeling of so much going on in the world that I don't know about or understand. During my retirement I may even try to figure out what the hell a debenture is. It sounds like something that the dentist puts into your mouth.

It's not like I didn't know people here. I know a sportswriter for the St. Louis Post-Dispatch. I guess I probably could say that I knew a sportswriter in almost every major league city. But I didn't feel like talking to him.

Of course, I knew a few of the Cardinal players. Since they didn't make the playoffs this year the city was in a state of gloom and I was sure those guys all had fled town for their off-season homes. There's nothing more depressing than hanging around for the winter in a city where everyone wanted to know "what happened to you guys?" It's hard to hide out for five months before you leave for spring training.

I called Tina but got her voice mail. Good. I really didn't want to get into counseling knowing that she wasn't going to do anything about it. My advice is always the same "Leave the scumbag." Her response is always the same: "I can't. The children."

I got to Lambert Field an hour before Alexis' flight was due. I killed some time at one of the newsstands checking out the latest best sellers, all priced about twice what you could get them for online. I had a cup of Starbucks coffee even though I can't stand Starbucks. Their coffee tastes like roasted tires.

I checked the arrival board and saw that Flight 337 had left Cleveland about 45 minutes late. To most people that's no big deal, but then Alexis isn't most people. She didn't take well to these sorts of delays, so I knew that when she eventually got here I would have to listen to at least an hour of invective about what assholes the people who run the airline are.

In preparation, I decided to go to the bar and drink my brains out. I had two beers. Combined with the coffee I made three trips to the men's room in about a half hour. Frequent trips to the bathroom is what life will be like in about 40 years.

I checked the arrival board again and it appeared that Flight 337 had made up some time and was due at the gate in 5 minutes. I headed down to baggage claim, found a good seat where I could watch for Alexis and watch other people. I never got to do that when I was traveling with my ball clubs. There was always the chance that someone would recognize me, but I had discovered that a player of my average ability could pretty much blend into a crowd and live life undisturbed. I didn't mind the occasional autograph seeker as it reminded me that I did reach some level of celebrity in my life.

As I expected, Alexis led the passengers from Flight 337 to the baggage carousel. She was rarely second in any line. It just wasn't in her DNA to be near the back of the line.

I knew she expected me to be there to greet her immediately. As I've pointed out, her patience level was about a 1 out of 10. No sense in aggravating her. I walked over and said: "Hi, honey. Glad you're here." We hugged. She kissed me hard.

"God, I missed you! Let's get the fuck out of here. Where are we staying?"

I told her I had made reservations at the downtown Marriott. On the way into town we had the usual "how was your trip" conversation. I figured I would let her get it all out and then we could get onto more important things. She didn't disappoint me. It was the usual, mopes who run the airline, a bitch flight attendant, a crying baby in the row behind her.

"They shouldn't let people on airplanes with babies," she said.

By the time we got to the hotel she had calmed down. We got in our room. As soon as the bellman left the room, she said, "Ok Tiger. Let's get it on. You don't have any idea how horny I am."

It was great sex. Afterward we went out to dinner. We got caught up on our lives. Alexis was at her best as long as she was on her meds. She was calm, cool and really hot. That's why I stuck with her. She was high maintenance, but the good times were great. We came back to the room and had sex again. Before falling to sleep she even complimented me and made the comment that I must have been just as horny as she had been. Not really but I certainly wasn't going to explain my overnight in Springfield.

"So how are things with Joe," I asked.

"Joe. Not sure I want to talk about Joe. I told you he's got a girlfriend, right?"

"You have a boyfriend."

"You aren't my boyfriend. You're just somebody I fuck."

"Thanks, Alexis. Just make me feel cheap and tawdry."

"Don't get all weepy on me. It's different. I never expected Joe to find someone else." She started to cry.

I didn't do anything to help her. I certainly didn't want to get into counseling, particularly with Alexis. That's not my strong suit. I also didn't take her remarks about my role in her life to heart. She said things like that all the time. Besides, our "occasional lover" status was just fine by me. What problems she had on the other side of her house should stay there. Not my business.

She turned off the waterworks just about as quickly as they had started.

"What are we going to do today?" she asked as brightly as she could. Bipolar? No question about it. I had gotten used to this. When she was on her medication she was the most charming person I ever met. When she wasn't…well, watch out.

After breakfast we decided to take a drive. Where we were going was my decision. She didn't care. When you want to spend some quality time with another person the car is a great place to make that happen. Other than listening to the radio you pretty much have to talk to each other. And, when Alexis is in a good mood, which she was, then our time together was delightful.

We talked about her job, my future, our careers to this point, our families, our various girlfriends and boyfriends. We talked about her husband Joe and my ex-wife. I talked about my sister and Bankruptcy Bob. I told her about visiting with Ted Dover and his family.

We took I-70 west to the Missouri wine country. Let me make it clear that I don't know much about wine. Beer is usually the choice of beverage in a big-league clubhouse and even then I'm not talking about fine ales and lagers. Usually Miller MGD is the top of the line, or Budweiser if you are playing in St. Louis.

But learning about wine is another one of those things that I've had in the back of my mind all these years while traveling the country. That's what this trip is all about, personal exploration. I think I originally read about this area in one of those airline magazines that you find in the pocket of the seat in front of you. I figured this was another non-confrontational opportunity for Alexis and me where there was little to argue about.

The Missouri wine country is located about 40 miles west of St. Louis along the Missouri River. It was originally settled by German immigrants. The area is like the Rhine River Valley back home in Germany. The soil and the climate have produced some very good wines.

I had checked out the website before I left the hotel and found one very interesting story about how Missouri winemakers saved the French wine industry. You can look it up.

"As trellises spread across the landscape, Missouri viticulture soon raised another flag of worldwide acclaim. In 1876, an insidious louse began a relentless assault on vineyards throughout France. The parasite had come from America and found the France roots particularly appealing-pushing the French wine industry to the brink of ruin.

"Fortunately, Missouri's first entomologist (bug scientist) Charles V. Riley made an important discovery. In 1871, at the invitation of the

French government, Riley inspected France's ailing grape crop. He diagnosed the problem as an infestation of phylloxera, an American plant louse. He found that some Native American rootstocks were immune to the advances of the dreaded louse. By grafting French vines onto them, healthy grapes could be produced. Millions of cuttings of Missouri rootstock were shipped to save the French wine industry from disaster. Statues in Montpelier, France, commemorate this rescue."

This is one of those pieces of trivia with which I can now bore the hell out of everyone at a cocktail party.

We cruised through wine regions of Augusta and Hermann named after the central towns and described in their brochures as having "old world charm and being unpretentious." Hermann was farther west so that's where I figured I would begin to test some of the grape.

The Buffalo Creek Vineyard & Winery had an appealing name and address being located on Possum Trot Road outside the town of Stover. They had some great sounding vintages like Buffalo Blood, Osage Chief, and the incomparable Show Me Red. Show me. Get it? It's a take on the Missouri state slogan of being the "Show Me" state.

We couldn't have asked for a better day. It was early fall, the sun shining, low humidity, temperatures in the mid-60s. Alexis wore a turtleneck sweater and slacks. I was dressed in a polo shirt but with a sweater that I wore wrapped around my shoulders in fraternity boy style, which, of course, Alexis had to point out. It didn't matter. She was gorgeous, and it was days like this that I was in love with her.

We stopped at five wineries to taste their various offerings. I bought a couple bottles of something called Mustang. I liked the label although it wasn't bad tasting either. The wine made us mellow and all life's conflicts were somewhat forgotten.

We shared a late lunch of cheese, fruit and wine on a patio of one of the wineries overlooking the vineyard which had already begun to turn autumn gold. This was travel brochure material.

We got back to St. Louis about 7 p.m. and headed for Dago Hill, an area known for its Italian restaurants. Knowing my baseball history, it was the neighborhood in which hall of famer Yogi Berra was raised along with his buddy and less successful major leaguer Joe Garagiola.

We went to Zia's "on the Hill." I had eaten there once before when we were playing in St. Louis and we had a rain out. This being a Saturday night and without reservations we had to wait at the bar for about 45 minutes before we were seated. We both nursed a beer. We probably had already had enough wine but it seemed a shame not to share another bottle with our pasta.

One might think we were bordering on a serious drinking problem. But it was just one day. Of course, the main thing was to not get stopped and hit with a DUI, but I had paced myself during the day and felt I was still handling it okay.

We got back to the hotel about 10, went to bed, made love and slept until 9:30 the next morning. After a room service breakfast, we checked out and headed to the airport. Alexis had a 1:25 flight back to Cleveland. She was fine with me dropping her off and not waiting around.

We kissed, murmured a few "goodbyes," "take cares," "love yas" and off she went. We had avoided discussions of future get togethers. We both knew this relationship was a day-to-day thing. Alexis had other baggage to consider in her life.

CHAPTER 9

I headed west again on I-70 past the wine country but my goal this time was Jefferson City, where I had lunch at a diner near the capitol. The place reminded me of where I had met Lilly in Springfield. Who knows, maybe lightning would strike twice in state capitals.

I had the BLT on white toast, with chips and a pickle. How's that for a middle America lunch?

Riding the buses in the minor leagues you played lots of games to kill time. Besides singing "A hundred bottles of beer on the wall" a few too many times, we played many guessing games. I was always pretty good at geography questions. Probably not good enough to be on Jeopardy, but good enough to impress a bunch of lowly educated minor league baseball players.

One of the questions I had to answer and won the 24 bucks that were in the prize pot, was: "name the state capitals named after presidents."

Jefferson City was one of those. The others? Jackson, Mississippi, Madison, Wisconsin, and Lincoln, Nebraska. I remember thinking that I had only been to Madison and I would have to try to get to the others. Now here I was in Jefferson City and Lincoln was certainly in my sights. Jackson would have to wait.

After lunch, with no Lilly-type action, I drove straight through to Kansas City. It was getting dark when I checked into a Fairfield Inn. I had an account for frequent stays at Marriott properties which owned Fairfield Inns. I also had an account with Hilton which owns Hampton Inns. It was always a tossup as to which one I chose. I liked places that served breakfast in the morning. It saved time not to mention money. I had more points with Marriott on their customer loyalty program and once you begin to see it build up there's just a tendency to stick with it.

I ordered a pizza to be delivered to my room, watched a movie on the in-house system for which they charged me $16. Then I hunkered down for a good night's sleep. I wasn't up to seeing the town and after Alexis I always found I needed a little time off from people in general. I had my itinerary for the next day all set.

I probably had played ball in Kansas City 25 or 30 times during my career. The life of a professional baseball player in a visiting town is pretty much arrive at the airport, take a bus to the hotel, hang out in your room until it's time to leave for the ballpark, spend 8 hours or more in the locker room, workout rooms, warm up, play the game, do after game workouts, take the bus back to the hotel, have a beer in the lobby bar, go to bed although sleep could be elusive after a game. Get up the next morning and do it all over again. Time for sightseeing was limited.

Hanging out at the lobby bar became frowned upon by the teams and MLB headquarters in the later years of my career. Too many bad things happen there. Baseball Annies, as they were known in the industry, would target players who are high testosterone guys. Both married and unmarried players fell for the temptations. That's one of the occupational hazards in professional sports.

So, the Fairfield Inn, a family hotel without a bar, was a safe place for me these days. Plus, the price was right.

The next morning, I went down to the breakfast room which was about half full. The TV in the corner was turned on to CNN. It didn't sound like there were any major headlines from the night before, more news about what the markets were expected to do that day, and a feature story about a family that had adopted 12 kids.

There were a few executive types with their briefcases and laptops. They had obviously come from somewhere the night before and were on assignment in KC. One table was occupied by 2 guys wearing denim and jackets that said "National Moving & Storage" on the back. It was clear they were long-distance moving van drivers. Out my room window I saw the van parked at the back of the lot.

I popped a bagel into the toaster. It was while I was waiting for my bagel to toast that truck driver number two looked at me and said: "Stub Rowe. Right?"

It was bound to happen. Should I deny it and say I was just a look alike? There weren't that many people here and chances were most of them could care less about me. They had their own issues.

"Yep. You got it." I walked over and shook his hand.

"Yeah. I thought so. We're from the Akron-Canton area. I go to a lot of Indian games back home. Hey. We're going to miss you. I saw that you decided to retire. Huh? Geez the Indians were lousy this year. Maybe it's a good time to hang 'em up."

"Yeah, it wasn't the best season. Time to move on."

"I'm Eddie Patrick. This is Dave Winslow."

I assume that's your truck out there. Where you guys headed?"

"Dallas," said Eddie. Dave, who was older, didn't seem too impressed with meeting a major league baseball player. He mumbled "hi" but kept eating his cereal and drinking his coffee.

"We have to pick up a load on the way back in Little Rock and then we'll be back home by the end of the week. Can I get your autograph?"

"Sure." The autograph business had become big in recent years. Some ballplayers and ex-ballplayers like Pete Rose never gave away an autograph. Those guys always get money for their signature. No sense in flooding the market. It's a matter of supply and demand.

I didn't think my autograph was ever going to be worth much and besides, I figured this guy would probably lose it before he got home to Cleveland.

My bagel popped up just as I finished signing. It gave me an excuse to break off our discussion and go my own way. We wished each other best. Dave grunted something that sounded like "yeah." I don't think it was anything more than that.

Kansas City is a nice town. That's the only way to put it. Believe it or not, I had actually been to a symphony there once. They have a great orchestra hall. We had played a day game and someone gave us some tickets and we thought "why not?" A little culture couldn't hurt us. I never bothered to tell Alexis about that. She wouldn't have believed it and if she did, then she would have invited me to some high-brow culture event in Cleveland and I would've had to go to prove to her that I wasn't totally a bumpkin.

My first stop today was the Negro Leagues Baseball Museum which is located in the same building, side-by-side, with the American Jazz Museum. I had read where this museum was always on the verge of closing due to lack of funds so I figured I better get there before it went out of business. Later on I wanted to get to the World War I museum. This was my museum day.

Besides paying the $6 fee to get in, I threw in another $25 as a contribution. It was a Monday so there were only about 10 other people in the museum. I had the place to myself.

The Negro Baseball Museum painted the picture of how black ballplayers and their fans were treated as second-class citizens during a period that they could have been contributing to the success of major league baseball. Everything they touched, fields, gloves, balls, hotels were always steps below the major leagues, or even the minor leagues. It's hard to believe that it ever existed. But, I guess America wasn't ready for integration. Now it just seems so strange how anyone could have allowed it to happen.

I saw the old game programs, the bat used by Josh Gibson, the "Babe Ruth of Negro Baseball," Satchel Paige's glove. A whole display case was devoted to Satch. I remember my father telling me about watching Satchel Paige pitching near the end of his career for the old St. Louis Browns. He finally was allowed to pitch in the major leagues.

Negro League baseball was big in Kansas City. The Monarchs were one of the top teams. In fact, that was where Jackie Robinson was playing when he got signed to his first major league contract with the Brooklyn Dodgers.

The adjoining jazz museum was more black history. Louie Armstrong was the featured display. Kansas City had been a mecca for the blues. It was easy to kill a day in here but the morning was enough. After a while your eyes begin to get strained from trying to read all the explanations on each display.

Soon it was lunch time and I asked the woman behind the admission counter for a restaurant recommendation. She sent me down the street to Arthur Bryant's Barbeque where the sandwiches were about a foot high between two slices of Wonder Bread. It was served on a paper plate with a side of fries. Maybe I can't do it justice. It was terrific. I didn't have an agenda or a schedule, so I decided to head back to my hotel room for a nap. The WWI Museum would be for the next morning and then I would head out of town.

Tonight, I would have a quiet dinner and maybe find a lounge with some entertainment. Something like a piano bar. Someplace where I could just sit in a corner, listen to music and be by myself. I could think some things through. I had had enough of other people for a few days.

I did think about Alexis. I tend to miss her wackiness but at the same time felt it wouldn't hurt to take a break. She needed to deal with Joe anyways.

And if I wanted to keep things open with Lilly, too, I at least owed her an e-mail.

Back in my room I decided to make a few phone calls. I needed to call Scotty and Nicole but it was too early. They wouldn't be home from school yet, so I called Tina.

"Hi, hon. It's Stub. How are you?"

"Kenneth! Where are you? Is everything okay?"

"I'm in Kansas City. Just doing some sightseeing. Everything is fine. What about you?"

"I don't know," she said as her voice dropped. "I just don't know."

"What's Bob done lately?"

"That's the problem. I don't know what he's doing. He doesn't really talk about it but all of a sudden, he's got money and we pay off the bills and go out for a big dinner. It's always cash. Nothing ever ends up in our bank account."

I didn't say anything. Unsaid thoughts hung out there between us. I wanted her to keep talking. If I said anything it wouldn't be pretty.

"Do you think he could be dealing drugs?" she asked me.

The idea of Bob hanging out with drug dealers just didn't set well with me. In my opinion he didn't have the balls to do that and hang out with a dealer who might kill him just because his name was Bob.

"I doubt it," I said. "I'm sure he's just having a few of his deals come through."

There was an awkward silence between us before she finally said, "Well, I hope so." It didn't sound like I had allayed any fears. She still had her suspicions.

"When are you coming home?" she asked.

I had to think for a minute where I now called home. Cleveland, where my personal belongings were in my leased apartment? Indianapolis, where Tina was living? Chicago, where my kids were being raised by another father? We grew up in Michigan but there wasn't anyone there anymore who meant anything to me. Our parents had died several years ago. Other family and friends had scattered particularly during one of the automobile recessions never to again return. Michigan is one of those net loss population states that is boom or bust with the automobile industry. The winters also wear people out. So right now I was reluctant to call anyplace home other than my car.

All these thoughts went through my mind in a mini-second or two before I answered: "I want to get to the West Coast, hon. I have a few people and places to see then I'll work my way back to the Midwest. My apartment lease doesn't expire until the end of March so I've got a little time.

"But I'll stay in touch. If you need me I'll be on the next plane."

I could see the headlines in my mind: "Ex-ballplayer Murders Brother-in-Law." That's about the only reason I would go to Indianapolis.

"Thanks for calling, Kenneth. I love you."

"Love you too, babe. Give the kids a hug for me."

The hotel had a small fitness room and a pool. I did a couple miles on the treadmill, pumped some light iron and then jumped in the pool for a few laps. I hadn't done anything of a fitness nature since the end of the season and I was beginning to feel less than lethal. I had lived a life of a professional athlete for the past 20 years. I tried to work out every day. At the most I may have missed two days without something to get the heart pumping and the sweat flowing. This felt good to be stretching the muscles again.

I got out of the pool just in time as a family with four little ones showed up screaming and hollering. The parents kept saying in louder and louder voices: "No running. Bobby, don't jump in the deep end."

Okay. Miller Time. I went back to the room, hopped in the shower, then laid down on the bed and turned on the evening news. The top story was about the GOP presidential candidate, Devlin Lester, who had been caught dilly dallying with the wife of his chief of staff and other women working on his campaign. He had taken nude iPhone photos of some of the women. What could he have been thinking when he did that?

Of course, the photos had found their way to a reporter with one of the newsstand tabloids. Now it was all over the network news. They were calling it "inappropriate behavior."

Lester is black. The woman, Dorothy (Dottie) Crotin, is white. The TV reporter avoided making the point that the interracial relationship, besides the adultery, was a complicating factor in continuing his White House bid. The photos said it all. Mixed race issues are not supposed to matter in our now enlightened era, but we all know that they still do.

In baseball we were used to it. If you had a problem with mixing of the races among your teammates, then you needed to find a different job. For the most part it was the black guys with white wives or girlfriends. But, there were also the white guys who really got off on black women. The Hispanic players flowed both ways. They were someplace in between on the color spectrum.

Lester is married with six children. He had been a Baptist minister before entering politics. He was reported to be in seclusion and his campaign was refusing comment until they could evaluate the situation. His chief of staff and his wife asked for the press to respect their privacy during this difficult time.

Right. As if that were going to happen. They never would. They were like pit bulls with the smell of blood.

Enough of that. I called the kids. They remembered me. We had a few "How are ya?" "What have you been doing?" "How's school?" "Do you miss me?" I didn't get very reassuring answers to that last question. The other questions were pretty much answered with "Fine," "nothing" and "ehhh…alright."

Oh well. I tried. I care about them, but the absent father thing is just not easy to carry out.

Loretta was her usual cheery and patient self. I knew she would never do anything to turn the kids against me. They would probably find reasons on their own. I knew a lot of divorced fathers. Many baseball players were divorced fathers. Several of the older guys were able to reconnect with their kids after they retired. I was hoping that's what would happen with me.

Loretta asked where I was, what I was doing, what my plans

were, when would they see me next? I could tell though that she was going through the motions and had other things on her mind.

We hung up wishing each other well. I told her to give the kids a kiss for me. That's always such an empty request when you think about it. How can you give a kiss for someone. It's not possible.

Suddenly I was lonely. That usually did happen after calls to family. I typed out an e-mail on my I-phone to fungirl1984@yahoo.com.

"Hi. In KC. Trip is going well. Miss you. Heading west. Next stop someplace north of Mexico and south of Canada. I'll be in touch."

The strategy was to keep it short. Don't say too much. I wasn't sure if I missed her or not. It didn't commit me to anything to say that. You have to keep your options open. I didn't know when I might be back in that direction and Lilly could be an alternative to Alexis. I would wait to see what sort of an answer I got.

That night I found a micro-brewery restaurant called the Ale House something or other. They had good burgers and some interesting brews. After dinner, I decided to forego the cocktail lounge scene, went back to my room, checked out the TV programs and fell asleep early.

Next morning, I was the first one down to breakfast. I checked my e-mail and found a return from Lilly. Her response was just as carefully worded as my original message. "Good to hear from you. Hope you are taking care of yourself. Maybe we can get together again in the future." This was building into a "keep your options open relationship."

I checked out of the hotel, then headed to the WWI Museum in Liberty, Missouri, about 10 miles away. I had not read much about that war but wanted to learn more. Like all these places I probably could have spent a couple days but felt three hours would fit into my schedule. You can only absorb so much.

To enter the museum, you cross a bridge over a field containing 9,000 poppies, each representing a thousand deaths. Nine million people died during the war. That makes an impact. The museum is filled with old artillery pieces, trucks and motorcycles of the era, tanks, and airplanes that to modern day visitors look so ancient.

A series of trenches have been constructed featuring relevant sounds so you can experience trench warfare. I would have preferred a Holiday Inn.

Each time I go to one of these museums I admire the museum-ologists, or whatever they call them, who put these things together. I feel myself transported back into time. You not only feel the experiences of the soldiers fighting the war, but also the lives of the civilians who are caught between the opposing forces.

What a waste of humanity. What were they thinking?

The special exhibit that was "Man & Machine: The German Soldier in WWI" tells the story of the Great War from the perspective of the German side.

I had lunch at the Over There Café! decorated with the flags of the Allied and Central Powers, a poppy field mural and music of the era.

Okay. Enough of that. It was time to hit the road.

Next stop would be Denver, normally about a nine-hour drive. However, I wanted to do a pass through of Lincoln, Nebraska, so I could check off another one of the presidential named cities. And there would be a quick auto tour of the University of Nebraska campus and its hallowed football stadium. That side trip would add about three hours making it an all-day event.

West of Lincoln, on I-80, the world becomes flat and boring. I knew about the history of the Trans-Continental Railroad which shadows I-80 through the state. Or should I say that I-80 shadows the railroad since it was first built first in the 1860s during the height of the Civil War. The North Platte River swings back and forth along the route as well. I remembered reading about its history in "Centennial" by James Michener.

I typically started reading a Michener book about page 200 so I could get into the story. Then I go back later and read the early pages because he spent that much time explaining how the earth was formed. Great writer, but he could have used a better editor.

CHAPTER 10

It's been said that old baseball players either become born-again Christians or alcoholics. Since I had already visited the born-again Dover family, my visit to Denver would be with an alcoholic. Carl Furman spent eight years in the majors. I played with him first in Triple-A at Charlotte. Then we got called up together with the White Sox. We both made a few trips up and down the ladder between the majors and the minors. Carl was a left-hand hitting first baseman who could also play the outfield.

He never passed on a post-game buffet or a hotel cocktail lounge. Every spring training he spent hours running in a rubber sweat suit trying to lose the winter weight. We all knew that Carl would eventually drink and eat his way to retirement. Looking back on it I had to wonder how he ever lasted eight years. No matter which team he was with, he had managers, trainers and the front office on his back constantly about changing his lifestyle. It did no good.

After midnight I pulled into a Fairfield Inn in Aurora, an eastern suburb of Denver near the old Stapleton Airport. Aurora is one of those stretched out communities that seem larger than the main city. Everything seemed to center on Colfax Avenue.

The night desk clerk's badge told me his name was Clark. He was about 22 years old and he told me he was a student at the University of Denver. He was working his way through college and hoping that he wouldn't be a late night robbery victim. I don't think hotels keep that much cash around since it's primarily a credit card business but some of these yokels who rob the convenience stores aren't smart enough to know that. You can't just walk into the Fairfield Inn after 11 p.m. You have to have a card key or be let in by the night attendant so Clark was probably safe. He could get his homework done during the wee hours. I wondered what the next day would be like in class.

After breakfast I called Tina and there was little news from that front. I just wanted to let her know where I was. I would call the kids later tonight when they were home from school.

Then I dialed Alexis.

"Well. Isn't it the big baseball star? Thank you for actually remembering that you used to fuck me."

"Good morning, sweetie. It's so good to hear your voice...too."

The best strategy with Alexis was to just ignore the sarcasm. I learned that a long time ago. Usually she would get tired of giving me shit and would return to being a normal human being.

"Joe and I are going on vacation," she said. "We've decided to see if we can put our marriage back together."

"Okay. Where are you going?"

"Why? Will you stalk us?"

"No, Alexis. I was just..."

"Making conversation. Right? You don't really know what else to say, so you make conversation."

"It's what adults do. Frankly, Alexis I don't really give a shit where you and Joe go. Maybe it's best for all of us that you two have an opportunity to talk it out."

I was tired of this conversation already and decided I would bring it to a close. What Alexis and her husband decided to do was up to them. I had never been anything more than a fling. It was time for me to put some things behind me. Alexis was one of them.

"Oh, so you don't really care about me…or us. Do you? It's all been about fucking hasn't it?"

There's something about the word "fucking" that people who are angry feel that is the best verb…or adjective, depending on the usage, to make their point. Now that I wanted to hang up and move on with my life Alexis wanted to explore our relationship.

"Where are you?" she asked me.

I thought about lying just in case she wanted to come see me. I wasn't in an Alexis mood. But, I just wasn't a very good liar. "Denver."

"Hmmm. Skiing?"

"I don't think so. It's only October. There's not a lot of snow yet. Besides, that takes too much effort. I'm trying to cut back."

We chit chatted for about 10 minutes about nothing that really mattered. She seemed a bit detached and that was fine with me. I told her I would stay in touch but I wasn't sure that I would and she didn't seem to much care. I was never sure when the end would come with Alexis. As far as I knew this was it.

I couldn't call Carl for a couple of hours at least. He had sent me an e-mail in the summer with his contact information. I had responded and told him I was headed his way. He was expecting me.

He was now working nights on a truck dock in Denver. Since he got to bed late…or early, depending on your point of view, he would sleep late. He was available during the day.

His wife had left him a long time ago. Carl had been in and out of AA. If memory served me correct, his wife had also. I think they met there. One or the other of them was always falling off the wagon.

There's a great bookstore in Denver. Or at least there used to be. With the state of bookstores these days I was curious to know if it was still operating. It's called Benjamin's Books. I had been there once before on a road trip when we played the Rockies.

I went down to 14th Street, a mall-like section of about four blocks where trolleys run from one end of the neighborhood to the other. This is downtown Denver.

Benjamin's offered a gourmet coffee bar. I always wondered if people didn't spill coffee on books that they were allowed to read and return to the shelves. After all this wasn't a library. You were expected to buy something. I got USA Today. Not the most intellectual read but it filled the purpose for which it was designed, a quick read while on the road to catch up on the overnight news, sports scores, and a snappy feature or two. I always enjoyed the capsule state summaries that gave you the impression that that was all that actually occurred yesterday in the entire state of Michigan, or Ohio, or Nebraska, where populations of several million people lived and did business each day.

The bookstore coffee shop is a good place to watch people. I remember meeting a woman at a party in Cleveland who was a 50-year-old widow. Her husband had died 10 years earlier of pancreatic cancer. She had stayed home to raise her two sons. When they left home for college, she decided it was time to get on with her life.

"I thought I would like to date again. I was still a young woman," she told me. "I decided to get a job at a bookstore where I might meet someone who read the same books as I did." She admitted to an extreme liberal bias and said she was turned off by men who would buy books authored by Ann Coulter or Bill O'Reilly. She had come to the conclusion that other liberals were buying their books online from Amazon.

About 11:30 I called Carl. He answered quickly, "Hey, Bro. I been looking for you." I could tell he had just woken up, his voice still foggy from sleep.

"Meet me about 1 o'clock. A place called Finegan's. We'll have some lunch and figure out our plans."

Finegan's was a pub near downtown. I found it without much trouble. When I walked in Carl was already at the bar having an eye opener.

"Hey man. Great to see you. Great to see you." Carl stood up and hugged me. He was a bear of a man. He could hit the ball a long way when he would connect. His problem was that he didn't connect often enough. And, he was "high maintenance." No one really knew which Carl was going to show up each day.

I settled on the stool next to him. I ordered a Guinness knowing that I would probably need to have a nap in about two hours. Drinking in the afternoon just did me no good. But, I didn't feel like I could keep up with Carl if I was drinking Diet Coke.

We rehashed old times. He told me he was divorced, for the second time. I knew his first wife, Mary Ann. She was just what you would have expected Carl to end up with. Blonde, at least most of the time, big boobs, loud. Carl wasn't the only player on the team she had been with. That wasn't a problem for Carl. He didn't really care about her previous relationships. Carl only lived for the moment.

I never met wife number two. He said her name was Denise and they had met at AA together. Neither one of them had stayed with the program. They drank together. Then they fought a lot and eventually went opposite ways. He thought she had moved up to Wyoming and was living with some cowboy type of guy near Rollins. He didn't know. He didn't want to know. He didn't care.

I asked him about his present job.

"Just something for me to do to keep the bar money flowing," Carl explained.

"You still got some money left from baseball, don't you?" I asked him.

"Nah. Mary Ann got most of that. She sued my ass. She got the kids, the house, the car. I was left with a snowmobile."

One Guinness turned into two, then I switched to light beer thinking that might cut back on my alcoholic intake. Carl began to supplement his beer with shots of Jack Daniels. About 6 o'clock we staggered out of Finegan's. Carl suggested we go to the Avalanche game that night.

"My buddy works there in the ticket office. He'll get us in," he told me. "Jock courtesy, you know."

Beside my better judgment I climbed in the passenger side of Carl's car. He said it didn't make sense for us both to drive. I was smashed, no doubt about it. Carl wasn't any better. He just didn't give a shit. He was a veteran of at least two DUIs that he mentioned to me. He hadn't learned his lesson. I was drunk but not so much that I didn't know right from wrong. I feared that I could pay the ultimate penalty tonight and end up in the morgue, another statistic of drinking and driving.

I've noticed before that big men like Carl seem to handle the booze better than normal sized people like me. He maneuvered the car through pre-game traffic and even pulled into the parking lot reserved for players, team officials and other VIPs such as suite owners.

The attendant leaned down to look into the side window. "Hey, Carl, how they hanging?"

"Great, Brian. Great. Meet my buddy Stub Rowe, late of the Cleveland Indians." He handed Charlie a $20 bill.

"Oh hey, yeah, man. How ya doin'?"

I nodded acknowledgement to Brian.

Brian pointed to a spot against the outer fence. "Take it over there, Carl."

We parked and headed up to the VIP window where sure enough Carl got us a couple tickets. The Avalanche were playing the San Jose Sharks. It was early season. Neither team was any good. The place was about 60 percent full. The crowd noise was lackluster. The Avalanche, like all the other indoor sports teams, tried to get their fans all pumped up into playoff fever with a loud rendition of the Star-Spangled Banner and a theatrical introduction of the players.

Baseball certainly isn't played with the same fervor as hockey so we didn't get many pep talks or pump up tactics. You have to have your wits about you. Hockey and football lend themselves more to the rah-rah stuff and throw your body at them as hard as you can. But, I just can't imagine that playing 80 games a year, the players can get it on every night. This was one of those nights that nobody seemed to get it on.

Plus, there are one too many in-between periods in hockey. It's like having two half times. Boring! Watch the Zamboni re-ice the ice. Go get some more beer. I started to fall asleep. Carl kept drinking right until we left halfway through the third period with the Avalanche up 3-2. We didn't care who won.

"Let's have a nightcap," Carl said when we were in the car. I was too drunk to protest. My head was spinning. My mouth felt like cotton.

"Sure. Why not?" I mumbled.

He hit the interstate at about 85. He was a criminal at this point. There was no way he could blow in a balloon and do anything other than 15 years in state prison. God save us and everyone else who was on the highway that night.

The thought did hit my mind. "What am I doing here? This guy wants to commit suicide and take me with him."

Carl reached into the glove compartment and pulled out a pint bottle of Jack Daniels. Like he really needed that!

At this point I was hoping a cop would stop us. It might save my life along with a lot of other people. Where were the cops when you needed them? I couldn't believe that we actually got off the interstate ramp without killing someone, including ourselves.

Suddenly we were at Finegan's. That's where the day had started and would end. And that's where I had left my car.

Carl headed into the bar. I got out of the car and headed to the curb where I puked for about five minutes. A cab had just let another passenger off at the bar. I waved him over.

"Fairfield Inn."

"Which one."

I had no idea. I pulled the card key out of my pocket and handed it to him. "This one."

Twenty minutes later after a couple emergency stops to let me puke some more, we were at the hotel. I threw a couple of twenties at him. "Keep it." I know I was slurring everything I said.

The same kid was on duty when I walked into the lobby. "Hi, Mr. Rowe. Did you have..." He stopped talking when he realized I was blotto. I waved at him and staggered to my room.

I fell asleep quickly although I woke up several times during the night for forced bathroom runs. The next morning came too early. I put the Do Not Disturb sign out and slept past noon.

A hot shower, a few cups of coffee and several super strength Tylenol and I was…well, at least I could walk straight. About every 15 minutes or so I would experience waves of nausea. As the day progressed they diminished but this still rated as a number 10 drunk. Never again.

I took a cab back to Finegan's to get my car. This cab ride only cost $12. I may have overtipped the night before, but who was counting? I just wanted to get back to the hotel. That cabbie deserved combat pay.

I decided that I had had enough of Carl Furman. He has a serious drinking problem and hanging around him wasn't any good for me. Besides, it was time to move on. That was my plan. I had seen enough of Denver.

I packed the car and headed west on I-70 to Grand Junction then dropped south on Colorado 550 through Olathe, Montrose, Silverton and into Durango. This trip through the Colorado Rockies is one of the most beautiful places I've ever seen. The color of the mountains seems to change with the angles of the sun. As I got into southwest Colorado the terrain was copper-colored. Life seeped back into me as I drove.

I stayed overnight in Durango. I checked into my hotel room, ordered a pizza for delivery and just hunkered down. I had had enough excitement the night before.

The top item on the network news was the report of a United States Senator from Idaho, Larry Farmer, who had been caught by a state trooper having sex with another man in a roadside park restroom. He claimed it was all a mistake. He said he was in the act of gathering evidence about the state's lack of maintenance in public facilities.

"I look forward to an investigation to clear my name," he said in a statement released by his office. "I am not gay. I never have been gay. Not that I have anything against gay people."

In the meantime, his aide said that Senator Farmer would be taking a leave of absence to receive counseling.

The next day I hit the road early stopping at the four corners where Colorado, Utah, New Mexico and Arizona have a common border. I did what other tourists did. I put each of my hands in Arizona and Utah and each of my feet in New Mexico and Colorado. I was in four states at once, for whatever that was worth. It's just lines on a map. Oh well, other people were doing it. I didn't look dumber than they did and fortunately no one recognized me.

I decided to skip the Grand Canyon on this trip. I had seen it from the air a few times. Certainly not the same thing, but I was getting a bit anxious to get to the west coast. Doing the canyon was a day-long trip. I wasn't sure what was waiting for me on the coast, but I felt the pull.

CHAPTER 11

I pulled into Needles, California, in time for a late dinner at the "Cattle Rustler's Steakhouse." A ribeye, baked potato and "the best salad bar this side of the Mojave," cost me $14 and change. Money wasn't currently an issue for me, but it's always nice to be able to eat cheap. I checked into the Best Western Colorado River Inn, "conveniently situated off California's historic Route 66" as the billboard proclaimed on my way into town.

After the night I spent with Carl in Denver I wanted to lay low for a few nights. But I also had mixed feelings about that. It can be a bit boring spending a days alone in the car listening to books on tape, mellow interviews on NPR, and the Elvis channel.

The one place I knew I could find instant companionship would be at a strip club. I checked the yellow pages and my only choice was "Hot's" located 6 miles west of Needles.

"Get Hot at Hot's before you get Hot in the Mojave." That was their ad slogan. I think they could use some help in the marketing department.

I took a drive out there. "Hot's" was a one-story building set back off the highway. There were lots of pickup trucks in the gravel parking lot. There was a small group of smokers standing outside near the front door. There were three men and a couple of women, who were obviously strippers on a break. They had casually thrown jackets over their shoulders to ward off the cool, desert night air. The rest of what they were wearing wouldn't have kept them warm in a sauna.

Inside a bearded giant guarded the door. He grunted: "Three dollars." He went 300 pounds easy and was wearing a leather bikers' vest. I was betting that his name was Tiny and that no one messed with Tiny.

Rap music was blaring from the sound system. One girl was grinding through her routine on the dance floor in the middle of the room. I made my way over to the bar, got a Coors and found a seat at the first row of tables closest to the stage. It was a small place. Let's call it intimate. This was a Tuesday night. There were about 10 other guys in there. Maybe things go "hot" on weekends. I was just looking for a place to spend an hour, have a couple beers, and watch a few pretty girls take their tops off.

The stripper's name was Sugar. That being her "bar name," of course. When she finished her two-song set, she picked up her bra and a few dollar bills that patrons had pitched her way. She stepped down and headed for me. I was the new meat at the club.

"Dollar dance?" That's all she said while pointing her boobs towards me.

"Sure. Why not? That's what you come here for, right?"

"Absolutely!" Her attitude perked up. She did a quick grind against my lap, rubbed her boobs in my face, then held open the side of her G-string. That's where I stuffed a five-dollar bill. Even in the dark she could see that Abe Lincoln meant a lot more to her than the George Washington she was used to getting.

"Thank you, cowboy! I'll be back to see you. Don't go away."

Sugar worked the room. A couple guys waved her away but most of them bought a dollar dance. Like I said, the place wasn't all that busy, so she was heading back in my direction before I had taken two sips of my beer.

"I've never seen you here before. I'm Sugar. What's your name?" she said, plopping down on the chair next to me and holding out her hand.

"Roger." I figured if she could have a bar name so could I. Besides, I was a minor celebrity. Baseball fans are everywhere. I didn't want to be recognized.

"Where you from, Roger?"

"Reno. Just heading down to Phoenix to see some friends and family. Stopped in Needles for the night."

I might as well keep making it up as I go along. "Roger from Reno" sounded good to me. It was catchy. I couldn't see any possible repercussions. Even if I tripped myself up what difference did it make? Probably most guys who came in here lied about who they were. I wasn't about to believe anything Sugar was telling me, so why should I tell her the truth? This was all a place of make believe anyways.

By the time Sugar had put herself back together a waitress, showing as much cleavage as Sugar, was standing by our table. I figured they took turns dancing and waiting on tables.

"Would you buy me a drink?"

"Sure. What do you want?"

"Tequila and tonic," she told the waitress.

The drink cost me 5 bucks plus a tip. Not bad. I've been to these places in big league cities where you pay $25 for a guest "champagne." But this was Needles, California. I suspected Sugar was drinking real Tequila.

We chatted for a while making up lies about ourselves and periodically watching the other dancers on stage. I figured Sugar was about 35. She wasn't a rookie. She was short, maybe 5'4" with a pretty good rack on her. She had black hair cut short, an olive complexion and a small tattoo of a flower above her left breast.

She said she was originally from Los Angeles and now lived in Kingman, Arizona, about 25 miles away. Sugar said she came to Arizona to go to college but made more money being a stripper. I suppose some of this was true…and some of it wasn't. Who cares?

While we were talking she pushed her leg up against mine and put one hand on the inside of my leg.

"Would you like to have a private dance?"

"Not right now," I told her. "Just thought I would watch the dancers."

"Okay. Well maybe later. I'll be back."

I was sure she would be. I was able to nurse the Coors for three more dancers all with names of precious gemstones: Diamond, Sapphire, and Crystal. I was impressed with their athleticism on the stripper pole. This really was entertainment. Crystal had terrific upper body strength. She pulled herself to the top of the pole, then wrapped her legs around it and leaned the rest of her body out parallel to the floor. There isn't one professional baseball player that I knew who could do that.

When you are sitting alone in a bar you think about all sorts of things. I wondered where you buy a stripper pole? Maybe the same place that firehouses get their poles. I don't know. I never thought about it before. I wouldn't think that you can scrimp on one of those things. You don't want it to break and hurt one of the dancers. That would be a worker's comp claim. I imagined the bar owner going to Home Depot and asking for the "stripper pole" section.

I kept an eye on the clientele. The traffic in and out of the front door had picked up. I suppose some of them were smokers who had to go outside to get their fix. But the place was slowly beginning to fill up with new customers paying Tiny their $3.

Mostly they were rugged looking guys in their 30s and 40s dressed in jeans, work shirts and boots. This wasn't the type of place where you spiffed up. A couple guys even came in wearing hard hats and tool belts which they took off and plopped on their table like gunfighters.

I couldn't exactly see the logos on their shirts, but their talk gave me the impression they were from a nearby construction project.

. There was one old guy, maybe about 70, who seemed to entertain, or be entertained by a steady stream of strippers working the room. They all made a stop with him and occasionally he would get up and follow them to one of the booths off to the side of the main room where they would disappear behind a black curtain for a song or two. He always came out looking like a happy guy.

There were also three women customers who came in, one with a man, and two husky gals who came in together. They seemed to be friends of a dancer named Mystic who gave them hugs. I watched as Mystic took her top off and proceeded to give extended dollar dances to each of the women. Mystic stuck her hands under their shirts and felt their breasts. Both women in turn leaned back and enjoyed the embrace while the friend watched and made mocking sounds. They stuffed more than a few dollar bills into Mystic's G-string getting kisses from the stripper in return. "Hots" was obviously a complete entertainment palace for all genders and sexual preferences.

Sugar was back. "Want to play with me now?" she asked.

This is what went through my mind. Sugar was kind of hot. I was curious. I was on the road. I was by myself. I was lonely. I was vulnerable. No one I knew would ever see me doing this.

It's not like I hadn't done this before. Living in a testosterone-filled environment for almost two decades I had been to a few of these places but mostly back when I was in the minor leagues. The big-league clubs frowned on their players getting into sticky situations at gentlemen's clubs. There was too much money at stake.

There was an old saying that "nothing good happens after midnight." That's when most guys got into trouble. But, now it was only about 10:30 and I wasn't a ballplayer anymore. I could do what I wanted.

"Sure. How much is it?" Even though this was a local place that probably had a price point that fit the community and I could afford it, I didn't want to get into an argument afterward and end up having a discussion with Tiny. It was better to work out the details beforehand.

"Twenty dollars for one dance. Thirty for two. I always give my newbies a little extra."

"Okay. I'll take the introductory special."

She took my hand and led me to one of the curtained booths along the wall. I was self-conscious walking behind her wondering if other patrons were laughing at me. As I glanced around I realized there was nothing to worry about. Nobody paid any attention. This was a stripper bar. This was what people did.

Behind the curtain was a low leather couch. I sat down while Sugar took off her bra, probably for about the 20th time that night. The present song was still playing so she sat down on my lap with her bare boobs about six inches from my nose.

"We'll wait until this song is over. So, Roger, tell me about yourself. Do you have a job?" I had to give her points. She was trying to make conversation. I'm sure she could care less what I did for a living. But, it was another opportunity to add to the fictional Roger.

"I'm a freelance writer. Magazines, newspapers, a couple of books."

"Really. That's so interesting. I always wanted to write. What do you write about?"

Her tone of voice gave away her actual level of interest. It came out more like "would you like lettuce and tomato on your hamburger?"

I told her that I wrote about politics. That was as far from baseball and sports writing that I could think of at a moment's notice. She didn't seem very impressed. All I got was a polite nod and "hmmm."

We exchanged more small talk. She "accidentally" rubbed her nipples across my face. She was working for the extra tip. We had a brief discussion about the size of her breasts.

"When I first came to work here I was worried that I wasn't big enough. But guys don't seem to care. The girls with the biggest boobs don't make the most money," she told me. "The ones who smile make the most."

Finally, there was an obvious break in the music, if you could call it that. She stood up, turned her butt to me and started to grind away in my lap. She went through her whole routine. Front side. Back side. She found new ways of running her various body parts over my crotch. I responded and the more she could feel me respond the more she focused her energies there. She ran her hands up under my shirt and squeezed my nipples then took my hands and put them on her breasts and squeezed slightly. I also got some hot breathing into my ear and little kisses along my neck.

The introductory special was pretty good!

The song ended. "Should we go for one more?"

"Sure. Why not? That's why I came here." I got more of the same for two more minutes. I gave her $40 rather than the expected $30.

Big spender that I am. She thanked me with a hug and a kiss on my cheek. I left the booth assuming that I had a happy look on my face like that old guy who I had watched earlier. My man parts quickly returned to normal size but I still had to walk between a few tables sporting a larger than normal bulge. I suppose that's one reason to keep the lighting in these places so dark.

"Thanks honey. Are you hanging around for a while?"

"I think I'll just finish my beer and be on my way."

"Stop by the next time you come through town. I'm here Tuesday through Saturday." She pulled a business card out of her purse and gave it to me. I had never met a stripper before with a business card.

When I got back to my room at the Best Western Colorado River Inn I pulled the card out and read it.

"For A Sweet Time – Get a Little Pinch of SUGAR." Her services were bullet pointed –

- Private Sessions
- Bachelor Parties
- Massage

Her phone number was 1-806-GOO-DSEX (466-3739). She even has a web page: www.sweetsugar.com.

CHAPTER 12

The drive across the desert the next day was pretty boring after about 50 miles of the same lunar landscape. Fortunately, it was an overcast day so the inside of the car stayed relatively cool. I can imagine that some days it's got to be beastly hot. It was good I had satellite radio. I figured it was hard to get regular broadcast reception out there. For the most part I listened to Cousin Brucie at '60s on 60. It took me about three hours to reach San Bernardino.

I was headed to Los Angeles for two reasons. I had an old buddy, Don "Blackie" Schwab, who was working for the Dodgers in scouting. In the back of my mind I wondered if I couldn't stay involved in the game a bit and pick up some cash by working as a scout. I wasn't looking for a full-time gig or anything, but something where they would pay me by the game report and cover my expenses. I could see myself doing this in the winter league and next summer.

Plus I wanted to see Katie Riley. She was a former Army helicopter pilot who had lost a leg in Iraq but was still one of the sexiest and most appealing women that I knew. I met her when I was asked to be a celebrity participant at a fund raiser for returning war vets. I had to show up, say a few words and sign some autographs while encouraging the audience to contribute money to the fund which was to be used to support vets with disabilities.

She was originally from Cleveland but moved out to LA when she got a PR job in the movie industry. Katie had gained a lot of notoriety doing advocacy work for disabled veterans. Other than for the missing leg Katie is beauty pageant material. She's articulate, too. I always thought it would be intriguing to end up in bed with her. It may sound kinky, but I just wondered what making love to a one-legged woman would be like.

I got into LA in early afternoon and took I-10 out to Santa Monica, exiting at Lincoln Boulevard, which put me just a few blocks from the beach. LA had always been my favorite road trip. I particularly enjoyed playing the Dodgers. I always thought the Angels stadium and location was too much like Disneyland.

Dodger Stadium in Chavez Ravine had gotten to be an old stadium. I know when they first built it around 1962 it was state of the art. But things have changed dramatically since then in terms of ball park construction. Even Cleveland now had a better stadium than the Dodgers.

However, it had location, location and location. Every time I played there the weather was great. Of course, we played mostly night games, so I would rent a car when I could on the morning of a game and go tour the beach towns of Venice, Santa Monica and Malibu. We usually had to be at the ballpark no later than 3 p.m. so I couldn't spend all day there and strenuous exercise such as ocean swimming before a game was strictly prohibited by our contracts.

But I was intrigued by that area and always told myself that someday I would be back and spend some serious time here. That's what this trip is all about, spending time seeing things that I couldn't when I was playing ball.

Besides Blackie and Katie, I knew a few other people in town. I didn't have much of a plan as to how long I was going to hang around, but I knew it would be at least a week or two, maybe even longer if I found something to keep me busy and amused.

I checked into the Golden Sands Hotel just a block from the beach on Ocean Boulevard. It wasn't by any means the best place in town. In fact, I kind of wondered how it had continued to exist on what can only be described as pretty high priced real estate. It had that feel of 1950s construction. But it was clean, and my room was extra-large. I had a sliver view of the ocean for whatever that was worth. And the price was surprisingly modest. I told the clerk I would be there at least three nights, figuring that gave me enough time to scout around town, see a few people and decide what to do next.

It was time that I checked in with friends and family. My first call was to Tina to make sure that her wacko husband hadn't gone off on her. It didn't take much probing to recognize the symptoms of a very unhappy person. I wondered if she was experiencing depression.

"I don't know what to do, Kenneth. Bob is never home. When he does show up he gives me money to pay bills and for groceries. It's always in cash. He doesn't talk to me. He doesn't talk to the kids. I'm not sure where he spends his nights. He comes in at two o'clock, three o'clock in the morning. He leaves again by nine or ten. Just says that he has to get to work."

I told her I would check in more often. I encouraged her to call me when she wanted.

"I don't like to bother you, Kenneth. You have your own life; you don't need to hear my problems."

"Tina. It's just you and me honey. Mom and Dad have been gone for a long time. We need each other. I want you to call me whenever you want. If you get my voice mail I'll call you back as soon as I can."

I called Loretta's number. I wanted to talk with Scotty and Nicole but I got the message machine. I left a cheery hello to all from "sunny California," and promised I would check in again later. I had been sending the kids a postcard from each of my stops since I had left Chicago. I knew I wasn't the best father material, but I was going to stay a presence in my kids' lives, even though they probably thought of me more as a distant relative. Loretta was a great mom. She knew I would always have the child support payments to her on time and I would stay as involved as she wanted me. Divorces are never easy, but she and I had made the best of it.

The thought of her getting remarried was annoying to me, but I understood. And, as much as I hated to admit it, Bill seemed like a good guy. I knew people who had friendly divorces and I was determined to make sure this one stayed that way. We don't have to be big buddies, but I knew we could all be civil to each other.

I decided to call Johnny Guererra, the head of security for the Indians. Each MLB team employs someone who is sort of like a private detective to watch over the players, who they are consorting with, what's going on in their private lives. MLB never quite admits to the methods employed or the fact of how closely we are watched, but we all know that it goes on. The teams have a huge investment in the players, a bunch of undereducated, immature and overpaid 25-year-old kids bursting with testosterone. Security's job was to try to get ahead of trouble and make sure it didn't happen.

A lot of the players resented security. They weren't easy guys to get to know. It wasn't their job to be friends with us. Most of them had been cops or had served in military intelligence. They were tough guys who had some funny stories about their times on the police force or in the Army but also knew how to keep their mouths shut about their present assignments and what they knew about the private lives of the players.

Johnny Guererra, particularly, always seemed like a good guy. I had shared a beer or two with him. He could be friendly, but you could tell he was always on duty. I thought maybe he might give me some advice about my goofball brother-in-law.

Johnny never answered his phone. You had to leave a message and then he would call you back. "Johnny. Stub Rowe here. Wondering if you might be able to give me some advice about a personal issue?" I left my phone number.

Asking for help usually got a quick return and I wasn't disappointed. Less than five minutes later he called back.

"Hi, Stub. What's up?" Johnny didn't waste a lot of words. I told him about Bankruptcy Bob and Tina and my suspicions that Bob was up to no good. "Can you give me any direction here, Johnny?"

He told me he had an associate in Indy who he would ask to look into the matter. He did tell me to plan on paying a couple thousand dollars for the service. I had never hired a detective before, but I figured I was going to have to pay something. These guys didn't do this for the fun of it. I gave him all the key information. He promised to get back to me in about a week.

I turned on the television to watch the evening network news. The big story of the day was right here in Southern California. A UCLA cheerleader, 22-year-old Marie Hatbender, had been found dead in a San Diego motel room from an apparent drug overdose.

It turned out that her companion, who had been taken into custody, was none other than UCLA's head football coach, Marty "Sugar" Cain, a married father of three.

"The Bruin campus is in a state of shock over this latest revelation," said the anchorwoman. "Lauren Gearen reports from Westwood."

Lauren was standing in front of an academic building. Students were walking past her in the background. "Thank you, Dana. So far, we have not gotten any official response from the administration. But I have talked to a number of students here on campus and most everyone finds this news to be shocking."

Clips of on-the-street interviews with three students were shown each pretty much echoing the previous one. "We'll have more on this in our report at 10. For now, Dana, back to you at the studio."

I wasn't sure how I wanted to contact Katie Riley. I had her cell number. I hadn't told her I was coming to town. I should have but I just wasn't sure how she would take my showing up out here 3,000 miles west of Cleveland. I sent her a text message.

"In LA. Would love to C U?? STUB."

I decided to take a walk along the beach. There was still a lot of daylight left. There's a cement walking path that borders the beach for several miles. During the day it is full of walkers, bicyclists and rollerbladers. I was dressed in shorts, a golf shirt and Crocs. I knew that once the sun went down it could get cool along the ocean, so I wasn't planning on going all that far. I headed south towards Venice Beach.

I went about a half mile when I came upon an interesting looking bar and restaurant called The Oar House. It was obviously a burger and beer place decorated in '70s camp with all sorts of memorabilia on the walls. I couldn't exactly figure out the theme of the place. I think the owners just took whatever junk they had in their attics, basements, garages and boat houses and threw it up on the wall. I guess that was the theme.

There was a long bar along the left side of the room with numerous Formica tables in various configurations filling the rest of the room. It looked like no one had made any effort to straighten it out. There were a couple of pool tables at the back. One was being used.

The place could probably seat a couple hundred people but at the time I was there it was relatively empty. The bartender said, "Sit wherever you want. I'll be right over."

He was working the place by himself, mixing drinks, washing glasses, waiting on some customers at the bar. I decided to make it easy on him and stood at the bar to order.

"Bud Light."

"Gotcha covered," he said. "Two fifty." I could see the flicker of recognition in his face as he made change for a five and looked me in the eye. He was trying to figure out where he had seen me before. Being a minor celebrity – Alexis would make sure to put the emphasis on minor – I had been recognized more than once. I liked to let people figure it out on their own. This guy had a job where ESPN was being shown all day long. Chances are he would recognize a lot of athletes.

I took a seat against the wall opposite the bar where I had a good view of one of the multiple TVs that were showing all sports. There was an early season hockey game on one screen. It looked like the LA Kings were playing back east against the Rangers in the Garden. The game was already in the third period. The advantage of living on the West Coast is that you didn't have to stay up half the night to watch the end of East Coast games.

The NBA had also started its season. Another TV was tuned into the Cavs and the Bulls who were going through their early season motions at a speed guaranteed to allow them to finish the year in one piece. The professional athletes from the different sports working in the same cities got to know each other. I would usually attend four or five Cavs games a year when I was in Cleveland. I was usually given skybox treatment if not a premium seat in the stands.

I had spent a few nights on the town with present Cavs star Joe Stanton, a sharp shooting guard from Texas whose primary bar trick was to down an entire beer in one swig. I watched as he swished a 3-pointer from what looked like the fifth row of seats. His shots had a lot of arc on them. They were always quite dramatic and picturesque.

I watched people drift in and out of The Oar House. It was a beach community. They tracked sand in on the floor. Most people were dressed in shorts, sandals, tank tops, cutoffs, and various types of headwear that ranged from baseball hats to bandanas to straw Panamas.

A group of young women came in wearing cover ups over their swim suits. They were perfectly coiffed. A dip in the ocean was not in their plans.

Most of them knew the bartender by name. Steve. He was working faster to keep up with the crowd that was growing little by little.

My phone rang. I looked at the number. It was Katie.

"Stub! What are you doing in LA? It's great to hear from you."

She sounded genuinely excited. This was good. I just wasn't sure. We shared small talk for a couple minutes. I filled her in on my post-retirement trip, how much I liked LA, and that I hoped we could get together.

"Absolutely. Tell me your plans. "

"I'm pretty open, Katie. No plans. That's the best part of this trip. Right now I'm just killing time in a beach bar in Santa Monica or Venice Beach. I'm not sure where one ended and the other started."

"Well, I'm just heading home from work. Do you want to get together tonight? I'll be hungry before long."

We made plans to meet at a place in West Hollywood called Agostino's. "It's a great Italian place. Pretty quiet. So we can talk," she said.

As I hung up I saw Steve the bartender approaching with another Bud Light. "Thought you might be ready," he said. "I just figured out who you are. Davey Crimmins. Right?"

"Wrong. But close." This wasn't the first time I had been mistaken for Crimmins. And I assume he had been mistaken for me a few times. We did look a lot alike, probably having some connections in the family tree many years ago.

Crimmins and I had played together with the Cardinals. He was still there and had just finished his best season. So, his mug got on Sports Center a lot more than mine.

I introduced myself to Steve. "Yeah. I knew you were somebody like that. Nice to meet you. We get a lot of the Dodgers in here and some of the visiting teams. I watch sports all day long so I recognize a lot of you guys.

"The beer is on me."

"Thanks, Steve."

"Hey, how did you know my name?"

"I see you on television."

"Oh yeah? Hey man. You're pulling my leg."

He asked for an autograph. Why? I have no idea. I didn't think that even with the passage of time my autograph would gather any value. And right now it was probably worth about the same as the ink and the paper. But Steve had just bought me a beer.

I finished the second beer and headed out. Steve waved good bye and told me to come back when I had a chance. "Sure will," I told him.

I made my way back to the Golden Sands, changed clothes and drove to West Hollywood. I don't know LA all the well, so I plugged the restaurant into Google Maps. There is so much traffic here I appreciated the GPS lady telling me where to go rather than me searching for all the street signs.

I found Agostino's just off Sunset Boulevard. They had valet parking, a concept that I instinctively dislike because I don't like other people driving my car, not to mention the price. But it looked like I would have to forgo my principles. It was obvious that parking was at a premium in this part of town.

I didn't see Katie anywhere so I sat at the bar where I could watch the door. Sitting by myself at bars was beginning to be part of my everyday routine.

It was about ten minutes before she arrived. I shouldn't say this, but…she limped in. She actually gets around pretty well with her prosthesis, but she also uses a cane, just to give herself a little extra support.

We hugged and kissed and told each other how great we looked. Then we got a table. I had always thought she was one of the smartest and most interesting women I had ever met. Plus she was beautiful. I just needed to get over this plastic leg thing. It's hard to put out of your mind. I couldn't help but think about deceased baseball impresario Bill Veeck who used his peg leg for an ashtray.

She was wearing a knee-length skirt showing one real leg and one plastic leg approximately the same color.

We shared a bottle of Chianti. I had the linguine with white clam sauce. She ordered the veal Marsala. I heard all about her new life in the movie industry and she heard all about my post retirement trip around the country that had no end in sight.

"It seems to me that you're like Forrest Gump. You reach the ocean, then you turn around and head back east. Then one of these days you'll just get tired of driving around and either stop where you are or go home," she said. "By the way, where is home?"

"That's one of my major issues. I don't know where home is. I know where it's not. It's not Cleveland. I just have an apartment there with a change of clothes. It's where I get my mail. Then again, I don't even get much mail. It's one of those things I'm trying to figure out. Where do I live? What do I do?

"I know that I should live near my kids, but I have to admit that I'm just not good at that sort of thing. Loretta's strong suit is being a mom. She can raise the kids without me. I sort of feel that whenever I show up they just tolerate me because a judge said they had to.

"And now that she's getting remarried, she even needs me less."

"Does it bother you that some other man could become the father figure in your kids' lives?" That was another thing about Katie, she had a way of just getting right to the point.

"Hell yes, it does. But he seems like a pretty good guy and I had my chance. I didn't do very well at the marriage and father at home thing."

I decided it was time to change the subject so I started asking her questions. She seemed to be in a great spot in her life. There's never any discussion of her missing leg other than in a joking way. "I didn't get to go skiing much this year." She never referred to it as a disability; it was just what it was. And, it didn't stop her from wearing skirts.

"Are you seeing anyone these days?" I asked.

"Nobody special. It seems that I have a lot of first dates." She smiled, laughing at herself. "I had a relationship last year with an actor I met at the studio. Nobody you ever would have heard of. He's a better waiter than he is an actor. There are lots of those in this town.

"But that ended when he left town. I think he caught on with some road show. I know it didn't pay well, but it was acting. We didn't have that much of a thing that he was going to stay in LA for me. I certainly wasn't going to encourage it. I think we were both kind of tired of each other. Frankly, the sex wasn't very good, either."

That brought about an awkward silence while I processed that remark. I could tell she was looking for a reaction from me.

Finally, she broke the silence. "I know what you're thinking. It's the one-legged woman thing. Right?"

"Not really." Yes, it was. "More just processing the whole thing."

She smiled at me. "Let's go to my place and you can check out what it's like to be in the sack with a woman with one leg."

I hesitated. This wasn't something that was on my agenda.

"C'mon Stub. You know you've always wanted to fuck me. It's just a matter of getting your balance."

I wasn't sure what to do with that comment. I felt like I was witnessing a car accident or some crime that came out of nowhere. How do I respond to something like this? I was conflicted. I always liked Katie and thought she was hot, but she's right, the leg thing was always there. I didn't want to offend her and yet I didn't want to pass up a good thing.

Finally, I took action. I signaled the waiter and told him we were in a hurry to make a show. Bring the check quickly.

A half hour later we were in her queen-sized bed. She had taken her leg off and propped it into this wood stand that made it seem like part of the bedroom furniture. Her leg had been removed just above the knee so she had a pretty good sized stump.

This was just two people who wanted to have sex with each other. We were both pretty horny. She was an aggressive lover who knew more than I did about all this. I forgot about the leg thing in a short period of time. When you think about it, not too much goes on below the knee anyways. She particularly enjoyed being on top. We made love on and off for the next three hours and then we fell asleep.

It was after 8 the next morning when I woke up. Katie was already in the shower, without her leg which was still propped up in the stand. I waited in bed until she came out of the bathroom, wrapped in a large towel and obviously hopping to get around. Her left leg had to be incredibly strong. I'm not sure I could do that.

"Good morning, love." She plopped on the bed and kissed me. "Wish I could hang around and repeat last night but I've got a meeting at 10. I've got to get going. You're welcome to stay. In fact, why don't you check out of the hotel and move in here?"

I went through the usual polite clichés like "I don't want to put you out." But I knew I liked the idea. Why not? It was just for a few days. It was her idea, not mine. She was pleased when I said okay.

I went out to the kitchen and made a pot of coffee while Katie finished getting dressed. She was in a hurry so it wasn't long before she came out ready for work, this time wearing a pants suit that covered up her leg. I couldn't help checking out her footwear. She wore stylish pumps on both feet. I would call them medium heels. They definitely weren't the tall spiked models. She gave me an extra key to the condo then poured herself a cup of coffee for the road.

"Got to run now, hon. I should be back about 6. I expect to find you here," she said. She gave me a quick kiss and limped out.

I could smell her fragrance for a few minutes after she left. I drank my coffee and thought about Katie. I could feel myself smiling as I replayed last night in my mind. I checked my iPad for e-mails and last night's sports scores. The Yankees were one game away from wining their 27th World Series over the Reds who were the surprise of the National League this year. I didn't have much of a feeling about it one way or another. I was retired now. I had embarked on a new life and a new adventure. I was aware of baseball but it didn't have a lot of meaning for me at that moment.

I wasn't the first one to say this, but "if it was so important, why do they play each year?"

I decided to check in with Blackie Schwab. I didn't have his number so I just looked up the Dodgers main office and dialed. "Good morning. Los Angeles Dodgers Baseball Club. May I help you?"

"Blackie Schwab, please."

"I'm sorry. Who was that? "

"Oh, make that Don Schwab."

"Do you know which department he is with?"

"Scouting."

"Just a moment."

While I was waiting I began to wonder if he was still with the Dodgers. The club had been purchased recently by an investor group and usually that meant changes in the front office, scouting and farm team management. The new execs wanted their own people regardless of how good the other people were. The industry was small and there were always plenty of ex-players around to fill those scouting positions. People like me, for instance. This was the only job most ballplayers knew anything about. They liked the life and didn't want to leave it. One way to cut costs was to get rid of the old scouts who had gotten some obligatory raises along the way and bring in your own guys who were happy to have the job at 50 per cent less than the other guys were getting.

There were a few clicks and for a moment or two I thought I had been cut off, but suddenly, there he was. "Don Schwab." That's all he said.

"Okay. Yeah. Like I'm a third baseman, you know? Can you use a new third baseman?"

He was silent for a moment. "Stub?"

"Hey man, how ya doing?"

"Fine. Absolutely fucking fine. Why the phone call? You need money or something?"

"And a fucking howdy do to you too," I answered. "I'm in LA for a few days. Can I buy you lunch?"

I checked out of the Golden Sands and by noon I was sitting in Shanahan's a downtown bar about 5 miles from Dodger Stadium. We both ordered burgers and some designer beer.

"Usually I stay off the sauce until dinner time, but I'm not going back to the office today," Blackie explained. He was headed for the Arizona Fall League to watch a few of the Dodger minor leaguers.

We shared stories about our times together and got caught up on the lives of some the guys we had played with. I told him about my near death experience in Denver with Carl Furman.

"I always thought that guy had a screw loose," he said.

"So, what are your plans, Stub?" he asked me.

"I'm just checking out a lot of things right now. This trip is meant for me to get my head together. But since you asked, do you think I could stay in baseball? Be a scout perhaps?"

"Is that what you really want to do? Sounds to me like you might be a little road weary at this point. I spent over 150 days in hotels this past year and none were named Waldorf."

"Well, it is the only thing I know. I'm pretty used to the hotels." There was a long pause and I asked, "What about your wife when you're gone that much?"

"Good question. Dottie and I haven't really been all that close for a few years. The kids are grown and gone. She has her interests. I have mine. Well, of course, mine is baseball.

"I suspect that if I was home like a regular person that we probably would have more problems than we do. We've adapted to the life."

"None of my business, but what about the intimate part of the marriage?"

"You're right, it's none of your business, but when did that ever stop ballplayers from talking about their sex lives. I occasionally have dabbled in the Annies. Haven't we all? Of course, as I got older they don't look as good to me. And certainly, I don't look as good to them. But the road continues to provide a few opportunities in that regard."

"So if I wanted to catch on with the Dodgers or some other team how would I go about that?"

Blackie explained the front office makeup and who to call. The head of scouting for the Dodgers was Mike Fury, a hot shot numbers guy with degrees up the wazoo. That kind had taken over the game. There weren't many Blackie Schwabs left. Blackie warned me that getting a meeting with Fury might not be easy.

"I'm working to change my scouting style. I used to look at guys just to see if they could run, catch, throw and hit. Now we look at all their statistics and the statistics of who they play against. It's all fed into computers. I have to do personal interviews. I have a set of 150 questions that must be asked and the answers recorded into a laptop. I'm sure we are missing some talented players, but at the same time we are probably finding players that we wouldn't have found a few years ago.

"It's a new way of doing things. For you to catch on you have to speak the mantra. You have to be a believer, or they don't want you.

Turnover is pretty high. There are always openings. You just have to be in the right place at the right time. Just like any other job."

Blackie said he would put in a good word for me and that I should send Fury my resume, in an e-mail, of course. We shared some other stories and parted ways about 2 p.m.

I spent the rest of the afternoon with catch-up chores like getting the oil changed in my car. I got a haircut. Then I stopped at the grocery store and bought a couple of steaks and other fixings for dinner. Katie lives in a townhouse. I noted that she had a grill on her back yard deck so figured I would surprise her with a bit of home cooking.

It was the right start to another evening of domesticity and love making. I wasn't sure how long this was going to last but I might as well take advantage of it while I could. It was clear that she was thinking the same way. It was pretty obvious that I was filling a void in her life, at least temporarily.

The weekend was looming. She needed to work again on Friday but suggested that we do L.A. Saturday and Sunday. "You don't have anything else planned, do you?" she asked.

"What you mean like going to the kids' Little League games or visiting the in-laws?" I answered.

"Smart ass." She was as good as her word. First thing Saturday morning we drove north on Highway 1 to the Topanga Canyon Road. Her leg didn't stop her from a pretty good climb to the top of one mountain where we watched the ocean far beneath us.

Later we hit the J. Paul Getty Museum. According to the brochure, the museum houses "European paintings, drawings, sculptures, illuminated manuscripts, decorative arts, and European and American photographs. It is a museum and educational center dedicated to the study of the arts and cultures of ancient Greece,

Rome, and Etruria, and serves a varied audience through exhibitions, conservation, scholarship, research, and public programs. The Villa houses approximately 44,000 works of art from the Museum's extensive collection of Greek, Roman, and Etruscan antiquities, of which over 1,200 are on view."

As we toured I had two thoughts – where the hell was Etruria and wouldn't Alexis shit if she knew I was at a place like this viewing…culture. I guess that's what you would call it.

We had lunch at a neighborhood Mexican place in East LA. It was called Julio's. Frankly, I thought the place was a dump and the area somewhat dangerous. Katie wasn't fazed at all. The food was great. I ordered the Enchiladas Suiza with a dark Dos Equis, just like the most interesting man in the world.

Katie went upscale with the Tilapia Veracruz and a margarita the size of a Volkswagen. I was kind of wondering how a one-legged woman would walk when drunk. It didn't seem to bother her at all. I began to suspect that when I wasn't looking she had poured some of her drink into her leg for ballast.

We were just having fun with each other and enjoying the day. We toured some of the usual tourist spots like Rodeo Drive and stars' homes in Beverly Hills and she took me to the studio lot where she worked and introduced me around to a few of the weekend workers, all of whom seemed under the age of 25 and were dressed as if they were going to clean the closets. Artistic types, I guess.

Sunday was pretty much a repeat of Saturday. We went to the beach for a while and just hung out. That night we rented a movie. Eventually, I had to make a decision as to when and where to go. I wasn't too enthused about the idea of a scouting job with the Dodgers or any other team. Mike Fury was not going to hear from me. I still wasn't ready to make a commitment to anything.

Just before we were going to bed my phone rang. It was Tina. I did a quick calculation knowing it was past 11 p.m. in LA meaning that back in Indianapolis it was 2 a.m. It had to be something important for her to call me now.

"Hi, hon. What's up?"

"Bobby got arrested tonight." She was blubbering. "I don't know what to do."

"For what?" I was thinking hooker sting.

"annnk rubbberyyy." She was losing it.

"What?" I thought she had said bank robbery.

"Bank robbery." That's what she said.

"Holy shit. What? How?" I never figured Bankrupt Bob had the balls to pull off something like that.

"What do I do, Kenneth? He's in jail right now. What do I tell the kids?" She was wailing. "Omigod. This is horrible. How could he have done this? He's such an asshole."

Her last sentence was one of anger rather than self-pity. Frankly, I was glad to hear it. I thought about jumping onto the same bandwagon. I wanted to tell her: "I told you he was an asshole," but I figured this was not the time. I'm 2,000 miles away and I'm her family. I needed to be the big adult at this time.

"He's in jail. What do I do?"

"Well, if he's been charged with bank robbery then he's not getting out any time soon. This isn't like a drunk driving charge where you can go down and bail him out. So let him sit there. In the morning, we are going to have to find him a lawyer. Do you know any lawyers?"

"No. Why would I know any lawyers? I never did anything wrong!" She was back to wailing. "What about the kids? What am I going to tell them? Kenny, I need you here. Can you come home? Please?"

"Yes. I'll catch the first flight out. It will probably take most of the day for me to get there so just hold on. Can any of your neighbors help you out in the meantime?"

She sort of answered me between sobs and wails and curses of anger. I think there was a "yes" somewhere in there. I told her to stay with the kids and let Bob stay in jail. She didn't want to hang up the phone needing to talk but I finally convinced her that she could fill me in tomorrow when I arrived.

Katie had been listening to my side of the conversation and had put two and two together. "Bank robbery?" was all she could say.

"The guy's an asshole. I can't believe this."

I checked the airline schedules and was able to get a seat on a United flight to Chicago leaving at 7:30 a.m. with a connection to Indy that would get me in about dinner time.

Katie and I talked until about 3 a.m. before finally falling to sleep for a couple of hours. We decided it was best to leave my car at her place. She had an extra parking space. She drove me to the airport.

"Well, this is the most unique excuse I've ever gotten from a guy when he decides to leave me." She was trying to soften our goodbye with some humor. I could see the same humor in this situation. We were stopped in front of the terminal. We kissed. I said I would let her know what was happening. She told me good luck and all those sorts of things. I figured that since she had my car we would see each other again someday.

CHAPTER 13

When I was on my Chicago layover I called Loretta and talked to the kids for a few minutes. I filled her in on the Bob situation.

"I always knew he was a snake," she commented.

"Innocent until proven guilty," I responded.

"Not in this case. You know he did it. If he's not guilty of this then he's guilty of something else, that's for sure." Loretta was not a fan of Bob.

I got to Indianapolis pretty much when I said I would. I rented a car and headed for Tina's. The kids were in the den watching TV. Tina and I sat in the kitchen and had some leftover pasta from dinner a couple nights before. She was blubbering most of the time.

"He came home about 9 last night. Parked out in front and before he even got to the front door there were police all over the front yard yelling at him to get down and calling him an asshole. They had their guns drawn. It was like something on TV."

I was thinking that they certainly got the asshole part right.

"All the neighbors came out to see what the commotion was. At first I didn't know it was Bob. I thought maybe there was a burglar in the neighborhood. The kids and I were all looking out the window and when I realized it was Bob I about freaked out.

"The kids realized it was him at the same time and started crying and calling out to him. They tried to go out the front door but I wouldn't let them. I started to hyperventilate. I couldn't believe what I was seeing. I felt like it was a bad dream. But there he was handcuffed, and they threw him into the backseat of the car and off they went."

"Did the cops come up to the door to talk to you?"

"Yes. A couple of detectives and a female officer in uniform came in. I have their cards here somewhere. They asked me to identify myself. I was crying. The kids were crying. We were just all freaking out.

"They told me that Bob was suspected of robbing banks. He was being taken to jail. I wouldn't be able to see him until today at the earliest. They asked if I had someone to stay with me and help with the kids. At that point I wasn't thinking very clear. I'm still not thinking very clear."

"Did you have some help last night?"

"Jenny Rozinski came over from across the street. The kids didn't go to school today. How could they? How can they ever go to school again when their father robs banks? I can't believe this. What an asshole."

Like a light switch she had turned from self-pity to anger. That's good.

We talked about finding Bob a lawyer. I volunteered to begin that process and as much as I hated to do it, I said I would go visit him in the slammer. I knew Tina could not comprehend the idea of talking to the father of her children through bars, or a screen or one of those plastic shields with a hole in it. I had no idea what to expect. I had never visited anyone in jail before so all I had as a reference point is from watching Law & Order on TV. I didn't know the jail was or how one goes about getting in. I guess I was going to learn.

I helped Tina get the kids into bed. She followed soon after. I stayed up and watched TV for a while, avoiding the local news. I unpacked, then spent a restless night thinking about my meeting with Bob.

Tina had given me the business cards of the cops who had arrested Bob. That was the first time I realized we were dealing with the FBI since bank robbery is a federal crime.

So I called special agent Timothy Lerner and got his voice mail. I left a message and as I started to call agent number two, who I assumed was his partner, Lerner called me back.

I introduced myself. Lerner was a baseball fan and knew who I was. I suppose he also knew me having the background on Bob. We actually had a brief pleasant "get to know" you conversation. He was professional about the whole thing and helpful.

"Mr. Franklin is at the federal courthouse right now. He'll be arraigned at 11 a.m. I'm heading there as soon as I hang up."

"Will I be able to talk to him there?" I asked.

"No. There will be no visiting until he is returned to lockup."

"What about a lawyer? Does he have a lawyer."

"I doubt it. The court will appoint a federal defender to represent him this morning. It's

all pretty routine. Get the charges filed, get the case assigned to a judge and set a court date."

Lerner said he could only tell me the basics of the case, which we also could read in the newspaper. It seems that Bob had lost his job about seven months ago but had never told anyone. He was spending his time each day in the library researching how to rob banks.

The money he would give to Tina every so often was apparently from a recent score. I guess that's what you called it in the crime world. Lerner said he was charged with robbing nine banks in the past four months. They were considered violent crimes because he carried a pistol with him. Fortunately, no one was shot or injured in any of the incidents.

Bob was looking at 15 to 20 years in federal prison.

I couldn't help myself but to ask Lerner how Bob had reacted when he was arrested.

"Broke down crying. Told us he wouldn't do it again and asked us to let him go. Talking about his wife and kids. All the usual shit we hear from guys like Bob who embark on a life of crime." I admitted to Lerner that I had always thought Bob was an asshole and it didn't surprise me that he was now probably a blubbering fool. I didn't think it would hurt Bob's case since he was already in deep shit. It was important for me to make sure that Lerner knew I was on the side of the law.

Lerner had given me directions to the Birch Bayh Federal Building and U.S. Courthouse in downtown Indianapolis. It took me about a half hour to get there. Getting into the building required going through metal scanners.

I found courtroom number 403 – U.S. Magistrate Daniel Bishop, Presiding. He was a tall, gangly looking guy who wore a pair of those glasses they call cheaters perched out on the end of his very large nose.

I took a seat and watched while three other defendants in orange jump suits along with their attorneys were paraded in front of the judge for various dispositions.

Then the bailiff said: “U.S. versus Robert Franklin, Case number 107848. Armed robbery of federally chartered banks.”

Bob was escorted out by a uniformed guard. He looked scared enough to shit his pants. He looked around the courtroom surely looking for Tina. Instead he got me. That was the best he was going to get this day. Our eyes met. He nodded. I nodded back.

As Lerner predicted, a federal defender in a dark pinstriped suit, who had just represented the previous prisoner, stood up on Bob's behalf, entered a plea of not-guilty and asked for bail.

The prosecutor gave the judge a few details of the case against Bob and objected to bail. “Mr. Franklin is accused of multiple bank robberies with a firearm. We consider him dangerous and a flight risk.”

The magistrate agreed. No bail. A court date was set for a week later. The case would be assigned to a judge. It was all over in about five minutes and Bob disappeared back into the lockup.

I called Tina to give her the summary of what happened. I told her I would head over to the jail and see if I could visit Bob. After I hung up I got a call from Johnny Guerrera.

“I assume you know the scoop on your brother-in-law,” he said.

“Yeah. I'm in Indianapolis now. Just watched him paraded in front of the judge. He looks good in orange.”

“What's with this guy?” Guerrera asked.

“Chronic asshole-ism.”

“I assume you don't need me anymore. You now seem to have the story on your own.”

I thanked him. We wished each other best and I figured that was probably the end of Johnny Guerrera in my life. At least, I hoped I didn't need him anymore, although it was always good to know where I can find a guy with his skill set.

As I drove over to the jailhouse about six blocks away I had the all-news radio station on just to see if they had a reporter cover the jailhouse appearance of Bob Franklin, local bank robber.

Instead I caught the latest political–sexual scandal. Dan Fogelman, Indiana State Treasurer, was accused by several of his female associates of inappropriate behavior. I had heard so much of that lately I didn't even wait to hear what Dan's specific offenses were. I switched to the all-sports station to catch the latest scores, not that I really cared.

I found a parking spot on the street about a block away from the jail and had to feed a bunch of quarters into the meter. I was good for two hours.

The security personnel at the jail were all business. There wasn't a lot of smiling or polite requests. It was just a simple "Empty your pockets into the tray, sir, and then step into the scanner." Full body, of course.

I had to sign in three times. My cell phone, keys, change and even my wallet were required to be left behind in a little basket that was checked in with a security guard.

After 25 minutes I found myself in a room with 10 other people sitting on plastic chairs. We were waiting to be called into a separate annex that was behind a thick glass wall where there were five visitor booths. I could see prisoners and visitors talking to each other on black telephones. They were separated by more glass that looked indestructible.

Finally, my name was called by a woman guard who was about 5'5" and weighed at least 260. She looked like she could play middle guard for the Colts.

"Number three" is all she said. I went to booth three and waited. After a couple minutes Bob appeared on the other side of the glass. It wasn't me he was hoping to see.

He picked up the phone. I picked up my phone.

"What the fuck are you doing here?"

"Good to see you too, Bob."

"Tina should be here. Not you."

"True. But, she wasn't exactly looking forward to a trip to the jailhouse to see the father of her children. Is there anything you want me to tell her?"

There was a long silence by the both of us. He stared at me. Angry. Then he started to soften, and tears began to well up in his eyes.

"Just tell her I'm sorry. I'll figure this out."

"Yeah, well, you'll have quite a bit of time to do that, won't you?"

"You're really enjoying this, aren't you?'

"Not particularly. I was enjoying my trip to California when I got an emergency phone call from my only sister that her asshole husband had been arrested for bank robbery. I took the overnight to get here. Someone's got to take care of your family.

"What in the hell were you thinking?"

"It's none of your fucking business." He then turned to the guard and asked him to take him back to his cell. He got up without saying anything more and left.

Well, that went well. Time to find a lawyer.

I wasn't sure where to start so I drove over to the Indianapolis Indians stadium – Victory Field and found the business office. Falling back on my connections in baseball was the only idea I could generate at that moment.

A young, fresh faced girl of college age, obviously an intern, greeted me at the reception desk. I explained who I was and asked if I could see the general manager, Dave Hogan. I had checked their web site first to see who had the position. I wanted to find out if I knew him. I didn't. But I figured he might recognize my name. He did.

"Stub Rowe. To what do I owe this pleasure?" He was about 27 years old. He was one of the new breed of wunderkinder that had entered the business with their computer printouts. I bet he would be running one of the big-league clubs in five years.

I explained why I was in town, as embarrassing and awkward as it was.

I asked him if he could recommend a criminal lawyer for Bob. I'm sure Dave Hogan, in his short baseball career, had not come across this request before. But to his credit he handled it without being judgmental.

"Let me make a few phone calls for you. We have several lawyers on our board of directors and I'm sure one of them can steer us in the right direction." He offered me a cup of coffee, sent me into a waiting area where I could watch ESPN and said he would be back in a few minutes.

He was good to his word. He gave me a slip of paper with a name, address and phone number. Dave gave me a little background on the lawyer – Richard Cramer – and said the guy was waiting for me at his office. We shook hands. I thanked him. He wished me well. The baseball world wasn't through with me yet, although I never thought it would serve me in a situation like this.

On the way to Cramer's office I checked in with Tina just to give her an update. I downplayed the visit with Bob, just saying that he missed her and the kids and wasn't sure of the next step. I saw no reason to give her the blow by blow of our visit. That didn't seem to help anyone at this time, although I was quite sure that would be my last visit.

Cramer's office was in a refurbished house about three miles from downtown. Several lawyers shared a space with one receptionist. Leather chairs and dark wood was the choice of furnishings.

Cramer was a ruddy-faced guy who was obviously a smoker. I could smell it on him and there was enough of an odor in the office to tell me that he would sneak a smoke in the building as well.

I haven't dealt with that many lawyers and certainly none on the criminal side. But he seemed to know what he was doing. He asked a lot of questions and took a lot of notes. Then he asked me for a $1,500 advance. I knew Tina didn't have that kind of money, or if she did it would soon be confiscated by the feds, so it was coming out of my pocket. I wrote him a check. He told me he would head for the jailhouse to meet with his new client.

On the trip back to Tina's house I began to wrestle with myself as to how long I would be stuck in Indianapolis. I couldn't just leave Tina by herself, but this wasn't exactly the plan I had for my baseball retirement. My car was in California and an unfinished relationship was waiting for me there. Plus I had to figure out what to do with the rest of my life. I certainly didn't want to become Bob's defense fund.

Oh, and I shouldn't forget that I still had kids in Chicago, although they seemed to be doing quite well without me.

I spent the rest of the day consoling Tina and trying to keep the kids busy. Neither of these activities is my strong suit. I called Katie just to update her. I knew I would not be able to leave Indianapolis for a while. She was cool about it all. She said she would find some long-term parking arrangement for my car.

Among the many implications of all this that I hadn't given any thought to was the fact that being a former major league baseball player and one-time All-Star I was still somewhat of a celebrity even as that distinction dimmed with each day I was in retirement. But it wouldn't take long for sports media to get wind of the fact that Bob was my brother-in-law.

Sure enough, before reaching Tina's house I got a call from a sports reporter at the Cleveland Plain Dealer. He had gotten my cell number from staff photographer Joe Dudek, who had gotten it from his wife Alexis. I briefly wondered how that conversation went. Joe was probably more than happy to give me up.

I had dealt with the media successfully over the years. I learned to say just enough to give the print reporters something to write about or for broadcast a sound bite here and there. I knew that lying did not work. They would find out the truth eventually. It was better to just deal with it up front and rely on the 24-hour news cycle to dim everyone's memory within a month or less. I told him what I knew. This story would headline the evening sports news in Cleveland, Indianapolis and maybe one night on some national sports news programs.

The story wasn't about me. It was about one of my stupid relatives or soon to be ex-relative. So, I knew my name and connection wouldn't last too long.

I was doing my laundry when Cramer called me with an update.

"I met with your brother-in-law. He's sort of an asshole, isn't he?"

"Yeah. It doesn't take long to figure that out. Tell me something I don't know."

"Well, I also talked with the prosecutors. This is what you might call an 'open and shut' case. They got Bob and his accomplice dead to rights. Unless something new turns up the only legal strategy I can see is plead guilty and hope the judge doesn't go too hard on a first offender.

"But he's looking at jail time. No doubt about that."

I didn't respond right away. I was still processing "...his accomplice."

After an awkward period of silence passed Cramer said, "Hello? Hello? Are you still there?"

"Yeah. I am. I didn't know about the accomplice. Fill me in on that."

"Okay. Your sister already has enough bad news to digest but there is more. His alleged accomplice is a woman with a shady history. No surprise there I guess since she's involved in bank robbery. Seems that Bob had a girlfriend on the side. Let me get my notes."

He was gone about 30 seconds.

"Okay, here's what the prosecutor told me - Alice St. John. 41. Past felony arrests for drug possession, larceny, bank fraud and prostitution. A couple convictions resulted in some time in the slammer but nothing of any real length. Has worked as an exotic dancer - no surprise there - waitress, office administrator and even spent some time in the military.

"Oh, and you should know that her present whereabouts are unknown. They haven't arrested her yet. When they went to her apartment it appears she cleared out in a hurry and hasn't been seen now for a couple of weeks."

"I suppose there's no way that Tina wouldn't find out about this as Bob works his way through the courts."

"Nope. Probably best she hears it from you."

Then again, I could see the end of Bob Franklin in the lives of me, my sister and her kids. I'm sure Tina will have a tough time seeing any sunshine but in the long run I hoped she would see this as a good thing.

"What's your plan for defending Bob?" I asked.

"I don't have to think about this one for too long. There's not much to defend. Plead guilty. Throw yourself at the mercy of the court. First offense - well, first nine offenses - married with three kids at home. Hope for the best.

"Sentencing guidelines are something like 15 to 20 years. Typically, he would be eligible for parole in seven to nine years. I'll work with the prosecutor to get the best deal we can."

"I guess I should ask you what all this is going to cost me? My sister doesn't have any money."

"If Bob works with me and pleads guilty, there are no other unknown factors that arise, we have a minimum of court appearances then we are probably talking 20 to 25 thousand."

"Okay. Let me know what else you need from me. I would prefer to pay this in installments so send me invoices as you incur expenses. I don't want one big bill at the end."

Cramer liked that plan as any attorney would. I went back to finishing up my laundry and trying to think about what happens next. Tina came into my room and sat down on the bed.

"I heard you talking to the attorney. What do I need to know?"

I gave her all the dope from Bob losing his job, then his efforts to become a professional bank robber, his accomplice Alice St. John and now looking at a prison sentence. She didn't seem to be shocked by anything, even the existence of Bob's accomplice. I think she had already prepared herself for the worst.

"And what am I supposed to do for the next 10 years? I'm not going to be the faithful little wife waiting for her man."

She rambled on for a half hour. I pretty much just listened occasionally nodding my head and saying "um huh" or something similar just to show agreement.

Finally, she asked me, "What are you going to do now?"

"Well, like you, this all came pretty quick. I haven't had a lot of time to think about everything. I guess I'll stay here with you a while to help you sort out things, but eventually I will need to move on."

That's where we left it.

CHAPTER 14

Two Months Later

The World Series was won again by the Yankees. I hate that team. Of course, I would think a lot differently if I had ever been lucky enough to play for them. I probably would have made a lot more money, too.

I've stayed in Indianapolis for two months at Tina's house. It wasn't exactly the life I was looking for but sometimes you do what you've got to do. Family responsibilities are not my strong suit, but I stepped up to the plate – excuse my baseball analogy – and did the "Dad" thing for the time I was there. Lots of chauffer duties and attendance at kids' activities. Tina's kids needed me more than my kids did at this time.

Halloween has come and gone. I've never been a huge fan of Halloween, all the dressing up and the crap candy that the kids get that just sits around the house and rots. But the kids love it, so I had to attend to two different families this time.

I went out with Tina's kids for trick or treating in their neighborhood. Then I hopped in my car and drove three hours to Naperville, so I could see my own kids in a school Halloween parade and some trick or treating in that neighborhood.

I've been forced into being a father figure in two families. It hasn't been easy, but I don't have a choice. I wasn't cut out for this sort of thing. I need to figure out what to do with the rest of my life. Walking the earth isn't working out for me.

I spent Thanksgiving dinner with Tina's family at a local Denny's restaurant. I know. Who goes to Denny's for Thanksgiving? However, when you have three kids under the age of 10 and their father is in prison, then Denny's is a pretty good choice. Big spender that I am, I treated. I think we got out of there for less than $40.

Thanksgiving dinner at Denny's was certainly better than in the federal lockup. I hope Bob enjoyed the Spam and cranberry sauce.

After dinner I headed north again on I-65, which I have decided is the second most miserable highway in the world. The worst? My friends who live along the East Coast swear that nothing is worse than I-95. I'll give them the benefit of the doubt.

I was invited to dinner with Loretta, Bill, Scotty and Nicole. Bill and I may be setting a new standard for current almost-new-husband and ex-husband relationships. We have gotten used to each other being around and I think that we are beginning to like each other. He's doing me a favor, when I think of it. He takes care of my family,pers so I don't have to. I contribute financially and show up when invited. I stay away when not invited. It all seems to work out fine.

Tina has applied for government financial assistance from the state. She was mortified that she had to do this. Tina hasn't filed for divorce yet but that's just a matter of time. Her lawyer assures her that the courts are quite sympathetic to an unwitting spouse of a convicted bank robber and philanderer.

She already has a new boyfriend. His name is Steve. He owns a small print shop and a UPS store. I met him once. He seems like a good guy. They met at the YMCA in a counseling session for bereaved spouses of criminal offenders. Steve's wife killed someone in a traffic accident while driving under the influence of alcohol and designer drugs. She's doing hard time in a state women's prison. Steve has sole custody of their three kids. I can see a blended family in their future.

Meanwhile, Bob seems to have settled into his new home while his case works its way through the courts. He looks good in day-glo orange. He has a cell mate by the name of Juan who allegedly is a major drug dealer and sports some killer tattoos. I would love to be a fly on the wall as that twosome work out their living arrangements. To my knowledge Bob has not yet been a prison rape victim.

I have returned to jail twice with Tina. She's terrified of going alone. Bob and I ignore each other during these visits. She also has not been able to get herself to attend any court hearings and she didn't want to be in the loop when Cramer called to explain how things were going. She only wants to hear the news from me.

"Just tell me what I need to know," she said. I give it to her short and sweet. No descriptions from the court room.

Tina put her house up for sale. Fortunately, it sold quickly. We've already moved her and the kids into a rented townhouse. She found a job as an office assistant that gives her the flexibility she needs as a single parent.

I flew back to California once to get my car. I drove it back to the Midwest in less than three days. The pace of this trip was a lot different than the one I just completed. I drove 18 to 20 hours a day, sleeping one night in my car at a roadside park. The other night I spent in a Red Roof Inn near Kearney, Nebraska.

Driving 2,000 miles almost non-stop takes a toll on you. I had never been a great sleeper, always dealing with middle of the night wakeups. It was a problem that had developed primarily due to irregular travel schedules in the minor leagues. It carried over to the big leagues. Ambien had become my best friend.

When I got back to Indianapolis I hit the sack and slept 11 hours, getting up to pee once. That's the first and only time I could remember a sleep like that in my adult life.

Katie and I agreed that we would stay in touch and maybe find a better time to pick up on our relationship. Since then we've shared one phone call that seemed a bit awkward for both of us, not really knowing what to say. In addition, we've sent a few e-mails back and forth but otherwise we've moved on with our lives.

I've been chipping in to Tina's family living expenses at a pretty good clip, not to mention the costs for Bob's legal representation. So now I was supporting two families plus legal costs. That was never in my long-term financial plan.

My nest egg was disappearing at a much quicker rate than I expected. I had never gotten one of the big-time contracts, so I always knew I would eventually have to find a real job. I just didn't think it would be this soon.

I began to give serious thought to what I could do. I went on line to check out how to create a resume and then realized I really didn't have any skills beyond playing third base. It seemed to me that my best bet at finding a job that would keep me within acceptable distance of my kids was back in Chicago where I had spent the bulk of my career and where I was best known.

That required a quick trip to Cleveland to get my clothes and personal belongings. I paid off my apartment lease up front in cash and the landlord let me out of the last month's payment.

I felt that Alexis and I had closed out our relationship so there was no need to waste any time with her. I had screwed up her marriage enough as it was.

Back in Chicago the business manager of the White Sox, Tommy Ferro, set me up with a sublet apartment in the western suburbs that had about three months to go. It was originally leased by a mediocre relief pitcher who had been "designated for assignment," as they call it in the baseball industry. What it really means is that they fired him. He was happy to get out of paying for the rest of the lease and it gave me a little time to figure out the rest of my life.

Ferro had seen guys like me come and go many times over the years. He was patient and helpful, but I could tell he wasn't about to spend a lot of time helping me find a job. Ballplayers weren't good at thinking about what to do once their careers ended. We are like any other group of people. Some of us were meant for blue collar jobs. A few had some executive abilities. But, while normal people were out building their careers beginning in their early 20s, we were playing games. We fell way behind the curve when it came to being of value to any company.

A few ex-players, with FEW spelled in capital letters, make their way into the broadcast booth as analysts and color commentators. I didn't know the first thing about heading in that direction. That was certainly nothing that was going to develop overnight.

Other ex-players have picked up paychecks by being a celebrity greeter at a casino. I gave that idea about 10 seconds of thought and decided to move on.

I needed a real job now. Maybe it would lead to a career later.

"I know a couple of outplacement firms where you can get tested for your skill set and they provide coaching. They can help, you figure out your next step," Ferro told me. "Some other players have gone that route and been successful."

This is what is called a hand off. Ferro just wanted to point me in a direction and shove me out the door.

I called the three outplacement firms whose numbers he gave me. I was told that it would cost anywhere from $6,000-12,000 for them to test me, counsel me, help with my resume and provide career coaching. The longer you stayed within their system the more money it cost you, so the incentive was to follow their advice, treat your job search like a full-time job, and get out of there as quick as possible.

All these companies had names like law firms. I signed up with Greene, Miranda and Tanner, Ltd., known as GM&T for short. Of course, they had to include an extra E in Greene. They had offices in Chicago's western suburbs not far from my kids in Naperville and the apartment I was renting.

I was assigned to a counselor who had owned a company in the safety equipment distribution business. He had sold it for a bundle. His name was Ray Horn. He had become an executive coach he told me because he enjoyed working with people, the hours were flexible, and he still enjoyed making money even if he didn't need it.

Ray had been successful in his career as a salesman, so he naturally pushed a career in sales. "Everyone needs sales people. Your background in professional baseball will open some doors. Some people may have even heard of you."

Gee thanks, Ray.

"Of course, being successful at sales is more than just having a friendly conversation. And you make good money."

I tucked all this wisdom into the back of my mind for further consideration.

Ray's job was to hold my hand and walk me through the GM&T system. I was like a baby bird being taught a new set of life skills. I sat through a day-long battery of tests asking me questions about everything from how to clean a carburetor on a power lawn mower to identifying composers of classical music. It was meant to pinpoint my unique skills and figure out an industry where I might fit.

The tests also featured essay type questions like: "What's your major strength?" and "Talk about a time you have failed at something." That one was easy. Having been a professional baseball player with a lifetime batting average of .268 meant that I failed 73 per cent of the time.

Of course, that experience didn't relate to a real-life job. I was discovering that almost nothing that I have done in the past 20 years related to real life. I've been living in Disney World.

The best one was: "Tell me about your five-year plan."

Easy – I don't have one. Ray said that was the wrong answer. I needed to work on that aspect of my life and career planning.

I was invited to group discussions with other GM&T clients. Ray or one of his coaching colleagues moderated the sessions. Most everyone else was there because they had been fired, or to use a less harsh term, downsized or rightsized. Going through that experience, their sense of self-esteem was in the basement. I felt like I was in a meeting of Alcoholics Anonymous.

Ray asked me about my knowledge of Microsoft Word or Excel. I sort of shook my head in answer. I had written a few letters in Word and once created an Excel chart of my own baseball statistics. But, other than that, I had never had an opportunity to learn these programs.

"Stub, you've got to get up to speed on those programs. They are the basic work tools today. It's not even a question I have to ask all these other people that come to us here at GM&T. Plus you are competing in the workplace with all these young kids coming out of college who know these things frontwards and backwards.

"They are creating their own web pages, tweeting, developing proprietary software. That's what the world is all about these days."

There were a few moments of silence as all this sunk in. I was beginning to feel worthless.

"What about Power Point?" Ray said.

I looked at him with a blank stare. I knew Power Point allowed you to draw charts and graphs, or in my mind, pretty pictures. But seeing as how I had little need for creating charts and graphs in my baseball life he might as well have asked me if I was fluent in Russian.

"How do I catch up on these things?" I asked meekly. This was getting depressing. I was seeing myself through the eyes of the business world. If I couldn't see a fit for myself, how would anyone else?

GM&T was careful not to guarantee that their clients would find a job. They made it clear that results were totally based upon the amount of effort one put into his or her job search. Their only guarantee was to pick you up, dust you off and provide knowledge of how to find a job and hopefully, a career.

This was all an eye-opening experience for me. It amazes me that more than 125 million people in the United States have full time jobs, if this is what they had to go through to get them.

My first couple days at GM&T I showed up by 9:30 a.m., which was early for me. When I got there, I noticed the place was operating at full buzz. The other job seekers were hard at work in their time-share cubicles making job followup calls, writing letters, scanning the Internet. Most of them had arrived as much as two hours earlier. The men were dressed in suits and ties and the women in professional business attire.

They were serious about this job search stuff. They were people with families that needed their financial support. Most of them had received some severance but their timeline was quickly disappearing.

It hadn't all clicked yet for me that I was in the same boat. Even Ray was in the office before me. I got the message. I felt like the new kid in school.

Ray encouraged me to start networking. "Go see everyone you can think of who are professional people. A cup of coffee. Lunch. A quick office visit. You don't have to stay too long. Just drop off your resume, ask for a referral and move on to the next person. Whether you end up in sales or not, you must sell yourself first.

"A job search is all about timing. A company might not have anything available this week, but then someone quits, and an opening appears next week. You have to keep pounding."

I decided I would start with someone I knew well. I called my old friend from the Chicago Tribune, Lee Crossland. Lee knew lots of people in town.

When I got him on the phone I discovered he was in a cranky mood. "What the fuck, man. I'm looking for a job myself. The newspaper industry is for the shits. I just took a buy-out. I've got three weeks left and then I'm out of here after 30 years."

We talked for 15 minutes and decided that neither one of us could do the other much good. We agreed that if we got together we probably would just drink our lunch and that wasn't an effective way to start our job searches.

When I had met with Tom Ferro at the White Sox he had suggested the names of a few members of their board of directors, vendors or business partners to whom he could refer me. I took him up on that. He was good to his word sending me an e-mail with contact information for four different people, all who sounded like they were important. Since they were involved in baseball, at least on a financial investment basis, they were open to meeting with me.

I reported in to Ray Horn on my progress. He was impressed. "Those guys are big hitters in town. That's a great start," he told me.

The first person on the list was Juan Pierre LeTorneau, an architect whose firm specialized in the restaurant business working for some of the major national chains.

Juan Pierre was rougher around the edges than his name would have indicated. I had him figured for some dandy with a $3,000 Armani suit and a silk pocket square. Instead he wore a flannel shirt and blue jeans. He hadn't shaved in about a week, but then that was sort of the in thing these days.

He was a self-made millionaire who had grown up on the south side of Chicago, a product of the public-school system, and had worked his way through architecture school at Illinois Institute of Technology. He had worked for a couple firms before starting his own company using a spare bedroom as his office. He became involved with the White Sox by being the low bidder on the remodel of their stadium club.

"In those days I was the low bidder on every job," he told me. It had paid off for him. He had moved out of the spare bedroom long ago to offices in Chicago's West Loop, an upcoming area of loft apartments, restaurants and professional services businesses. LeTorneau & Associates was teeming with more than 100 architects and associates, all dressed like him, working on projects around the world. I was the only wearing a tie and unemployed.

I was beginning to wonder if his name was really Juan Pierre LeTorneau. A name like Joe Grobowski would have fit him better.

I could tell that Juan Pierre didn't mean to be condescending towards me. But when he started asking questions about my business experiences it became embarrassing since I had none.

"Didn't you work someplace during the offseason?" he asked.

"No. Baseball is a full-time job. I was working out in a gym and taking indoor batting practice. There are only about four months between the end of a season until the next season started. It wasn't like I was going to find a real job during that period."

"Uh huh." I could tell he was trying to be helpful. I think it was dawning on him, and me, how unprepared I was in the workplace at age 36. He suggested that I consider management trainee programs with restaurant chains.

Okay. Well, thanks for the cup of coffee, Juan Pierre.

Unfortunately, that's was a precursor of how things were going to go for the next couple of weeks. I was coming to the realization that I was essentially unemployable.

Being a casino celebrity greeter may be my future after all.

Since I was close by I made it a point to be involved in the life of my kids, more than I had ever been before. Loretta was fine with it. I took turns with Loretta and Bill in taking the kids to school in the morning or picking them after. They were getting involved in a lot of weekend sports teams, so I was there. I did my best not to interfere with their regular family life. I was invited over for dinner a few times. Loretta and I got along now better than we had in years.

She and Bill were also supportive of my job search providing suggestions of people to meet with and offering a boost to my shattered ego. This wasn't easy on a guy who spent most of his adult life in the spotlight of professional sports.

Among the people I met with during the next few weeks were the executive directors of two local chambers of commerce, an attorney involved with startup companies, a real estate developer, an insurance broker, the president of a regional bank, the human resources director of a food distributor and a couple of rich guys who invested in all sorts of companies.

As instructed by Ray, I was not supposed to treat any of these meetings as an official job interview. They were all networking opportunities that he assured me would eventually lead to a real job.

"These people are connected. They hear things. They see opportunities. They are involved in the business community. Make a good impression and they'll remember you. If you come off like a knucklehead...then forget it."

My biggest concern was that I just didn't think I had any marketable skills.

I found that my little bit of celebrity did help in getting appointments. That was the good news. The bad news was that most people just wanted to talk baseball with me and didn't seem to take me seriously as someone who could be successful in business.

My associates at GM&T seemed envious and a bit pissed off that I could get into see these people and they couldn't. I couldn't blame them. They were much more qualified than me.

The Chicago winter had set in. Dealing with the snow and cold became a challenge shoveling the snow off my car and chipping the ice off the windshield. I had forgotten what it was like to live in the north throughout the winter without spring training looming just a few weeks away in Arizona or Florida. I had always reported early just to get away from this weather.

Instead of going to GM&T to work on my interviewing skills I would have preferred to stay home and watch Judge Judy. But I kept showing up to meet with Ray and the other pitiful job seekers.

On the family front, when asked I drove the kids to school in the morning and did the evening pickup as well. Loretta and Bill appreciated my willingness to chip in while at the same time I was careful not to overstay my welcome. Maybe they thought that it was good to have an ex-husband around the house, as long as I made my child support payments on time.

I was also going back and forth to Indianapolis, sending Tina and her attorney money. I was trying to adjust to life without the next baseball season on the horizon. Frankly, I've never been so bored in my life. Where was this all going?

I kept a close eye on my diminishing bank account that not all that long ago seemed robust and able to keep me in a lifestyle to which I had become accustomed. Now I was beginning to feel the pressure to get some revenue coming in again. I had this fear of becoming one of the statistics that I had been warned about, the ex-jock who files for bankruptcy five years after hanging up his cleats.

I kept in touch with my baseball friends and a few of them called me to check in. I read every issue of Baseball America to keep up with what was going on in the industry. It was during the off-season when all the free agent news was made.

My good friend Frankie Laporte was headed back to the Indians on a two-year contract. He was one of those pitchers who never had to throw too hard relying more on location and change of speeds. Managers always saw him as a spot player pitching out of the bullpen to a couple of batters at a time. His arm would last forever.

Indians manager Charlie Barlow got the ax the day after the season ended. But, having been in all levels of baseball for the past four decades he had a gazillion friends and was rehired as a coach with the Houston Astros a week later. Charlie was the ultimate baseball lifer who wasn't fussy about where he spent the baseball season. Everyone knew he was available and they respected his knowledge of the game.

I was surprised that Elton Woodard survived as general manager of the Indians. In fact, he got an extension on his contract.

CHAPTER

15

March in Arizona

Winter and a career in Chicago weren't working out for me. I had gotten a couple of sympathy job offers. I accepted a position as a management trainee with Second Cortland Bank and Trust Company of Illinois. I have no idea whatever happened to the First Cortland Bank.

They hire 10 new bankers twice a year with the idea that, after one year, one out of 10 would make it. In my training class I was the oldest by about 15 years. The rest of them had just graduated from college. I felt like the kid in school who gets held back a grade or two. In my case it was like a decade and a half.

My boss liked the idea of having an ex-jock around to talk baseball with clients. We would go into a meeting and he would introduce me: "This is my associate Stub Rowe. You remember Stub from when he played with the White Sox." For some reason he always spoke a little louder when he introduced me. I guess he wanted to make sure that the client knew he was talking to Stub Rowe, ex-major leaguer.

I could tell that the client usually had been tipped off in advance because he would respond with some platitude about how much he liked watching me play. Usually a ten-minute discussion about the upcoming season would ensue before we got down to banking business during which I would sit there and try to look interested.

My boss never took me on calls when the client was a woman. I guess he figured I wouldn't have the same connection with women. Pretty sexist, if you ask me.

The more discussions I had about baseball the more I missed my old life. Banking was tedious and boring. I quit after three weeks.

Fulfilling my fatherly duties also began to wear on me. I just wasn't very good at that whole thing. Sorry, kids. I'm a better father when I show up every now and then. Plus I knew that even a cooperative ex-husband has a certain amount of shelf life before it was time to disappear. I had overstayed my expiration date.

One freezing day at the end of January I called Elton Woodard. Teams had long ago locked up their spring training staffs, but one thing I learned from Ray Horn is that you never know when an opening may occur.

"Kenneth?" Elton boomed in his big voice. "Your timing is perfect my boy. It just so happens that one of our spring instructors had to drop out. His wife was diagnosed with cancer. He needs to stay home and take care of her.

"I can offer you room and board and $800 a week for sixweeks and maybe a little longer if you are willing to hang around for extended spring training."

"Is that what the other instructors get?" I asked.

He paused. I heard him take a deep breath as he considered his response.

"You're a rookie again, Kenneth. You need a job. Don't push it. If things work out we might find something else for you down the road."

I took the job as he knew I would. I'm working with the low minor leaguers in their first or second spring training. They are all 19 to 22 years old. My job primarily is to hit thousands of ground balls to infield prospects, fly balls to the outfielders, pitch some batting practice and provide veteran insight on how to be a successful major league baseball player.

I've gotten pretty good using the fungo bat. That's a bat that is lighter and longer than the bat used in games. It's made specifically for facilitating infield and outfield drills. It sort of looks like a cross between a bat and a broomstick.

The club provided housing in a local economy hotel. I share a room with another rookie coach. Tom Alford was a career minor leaguer. He's gung-ho about this job and has his sights set on managing some day in the majors.

Tom had been a catcher. He spent seven years in trying to get past Double-A ball playing in the farm systems for the Rangers and Mariners as well as a couple stints in the independent leagues. All ex-catchers think they should be managers.

"There are more major league managers who were catchers than from any other position," he told me several times. "We have an ability to see the whole field and learn how to manage a game." He was willing to spend as much time as it took in the bus leagues to make it to the varsity team. That had been his baseball life as a player, so he wasn't used to anything better.

I was still trying to get used to the fact that I was starting over at the bottom. It would probably do me some good to catch his spark.

I guess I've shown a good enough attitude, however, to make the cut. Elton called and offered me a position as the hitting coach with the Indians' rookie team in Bluefield, West Virginia. He offered me a raise to $1,500 a month plus a housing allowance.

That season doesn't start until June after the free agent draft which gives teams time to sign players just graduating from high school or college who will comprise the rookie league team.

I will stay in Arizona working with the injured players who are left behind to rehabilitate and the players under contract who haven't yet received a season assignment. Most of them will never make it out of Class A ball but they have their dreams.

There will also be a new contingent of players arriving from the Dominican Republic and other Caribbean countries who will need guidance in living and playing baseball in the United States. Some of these kids are as young as16 and 17 and not only need baseball instruction but some of the other life skills that we take for granted such as personal hygiene, finance and how to order dinner in a restaurant.

They have been raised in impoverished countries and this is their opportunity to improve their lives and those of their families. For the most part they are superb athletes who just need to hone their skills to make it to the big leagues.

The team employs a couple of Spanish interpreters. It would be impossible for us to do without them, although on the field I find that they instinctively do the right thing without verbal instruction. They have been playing baseball since they could walk.

I've stayed in touch with Tina and her lawyer via e-mail and I make it a point to call once a week. Bankrupt Bob pleaded guilty and got a new client discount of 15 years in prison. The prosecution had recommended 20 years. He's eligible for parole in eight years. He's serving his time at the Danbury Correctional Institute in Connecticut. His accomplice, or who I like to call his gun moll, Alice St. John, is a still a fugitive. Her last confirmed sighting was a grainy video as she was crossing the border into Mexico at Matamoros.

"Are you going to visit Bob?" I asked Tina.

"Are you crazy? I don't do prisons, and neither do my kids. He created his life for himself. He can live it by himself."

I've been writing letters and sending postcards to my kids each week. This is a throwback to something that was done in a prior century before e-mail. But, at their ages of 7 and 5 they don't have e-mail accounts. My messages are short and sweet and meant for their mother to read to them.

Once a month I send them a small gift. Thank you, Amazon, for being there when I need you.

In my 16 years in professional baseball I never saw myself as being a baseball lifer. But that's the road I'm on now. It's home for me.

"Hey. Heads up out there," I yell to some 20-year-old infielder before hitting another grounder to him. My fungo bat feels like a wand must feel to a symphony conductor. "Bring it home now! Good throw! That's it!"

I ended my playing career with a ground ball to the second baseman. I'm starting my new career the same way.

Acknowledgments

It took me 8 years to write this novel. I started it while in between professional opportunities. I completed about 75 percent but then went back to work and it wasn't until I retired for good almost 7 years later that I was able to put the finishing touches on it.

Two author friends – Bob Goldsborough and Russ Fee – were my inspirations to finally get this manuscript across the goal line. I found myself embarrassed when we would have lunch and share writing stories that they each were working on novels 4, 5 or 6 while I was struggling to finish one. Thanks guys for shaming me into it.

Long-time friend Bill Donohue, who I served with in the U.S. Marine Corps, was the first to read a draft. Bill is the fastest reader I know so I got feedback in one weekend. Thanks Bill for your friendship and your support.

Richard Rotman was my second reader. He mentored me on my first two days on the job as a reporter at the City News Bureau of Chicago in 1970. It seemed appropriate that he would be there for me again in reviewing my first novel. Thanks Rich.

Both Rich and I were fortunate to have learned from Paul Zimbrakos, truly a great editor and friend at City News Bureau of Chicago. Paul guided many hundreds, if not thousands, of young journalists through their first jobs on the beat.

Don Kopriva provided the final editing and wordsmithing, a service he so ably provided to me for 16 years when we worked together publishing a local business newspaper.

And a special thanks to the memory of the late Dr. Ken Macrorie, my creative writing professor at Western Michigan University, who was the first person to teach me the mechanics of writing for an audience. His lessons prevail to this day whenever I sit down at the keyboard.

And most of all, thanks to Pat – my best friend, life partner and helpmate. You keep me grounded and moving forward through all these years together.

About the Author

James Elsener grew up in southern Michigan. After high school he enlisted in the United States Marine Corps serving for four and half years on active duty including a tour in Vietnam.

After graduation from Western Michigan University he got his first journalism job as a reporter with the City News Bureau of Chicago. He then worked for 5 years at the Chicago Tribune as a business reporter.

Elsener went on to manage the national trade association – Suburban Newspapers of America. He and his wife Pat launched their own area business newspaper – The Business Ledger, which was later sold to a Chicago area daily newspaper company.

He is now writing books and living in River Forest, Illinois.

Made in the USA
San Bernardino, CA
18 August 2018